God's Gifts To Us All

By

Michael S. Brown

First Edition

Published By
Bluebird Meadows
Stevensville, Michigan

$24.^{95}$ Suggested Retail
USA

Copyright © 1997 Michael S. Brown

All rights reserved. No part of this book shall be reproduced, copied, electronically scanned, stored, recorded, or otherwise used without written permission of the author.

God's Gift To Us All is a fictional book about fictional characters. Any resemblance between characters in this book and real people, living or dead, is purely coincidental.

International Standard Book Number: Pending

Library of Congress Catalog Card Number: 97-94426

Printed With Pride In The United States Of America

About The Cover

Among the works of the earliest Americans is an ancient sun diagram etched in stone. A section of the petroglyph looks something like this:

This simple diagram has always impressed me. I read its flow from lower left to upper right. My interpretation has been that life presents points of change. If we don't change, or make the wrong change, the future is short, represented by a single sun. On the other hand, if we are able to make the correct change, the future is long, represented by many suns. I feel this diagram works for individuals as well as societies and civilizations.

Most people look upon this ancient art as being part of primitive societies. Maybe this primitive diagram holds the wisdom to show us the way to a better future. The symbol on the cover is a tribute to the author of this work of art.

I feel this diagram can model our values and beliefs. If we view our values and beliefs objectively, we can see many are reflections of our heritage. Rigidly continuing our traditional thoughts in an ever-changing society may not be the best pathway to the future. Some strategic changes may be in our best interest.

While *God's Gifts To Us All* is a fictional book about what God is and how God 'works', *God's Gifts To Us All* is also about values and beliefs. It is a book about personal change. This book alone may not reshape value systems; perhaps it can precipitate the first steps down a new road to the future.

Are we standing at a fork in the road? Are we wise enough to select the best route? If we just coast along, our future may not be very bright.

A society is made of its individuals. What values and beliefs will YOU pass along to the next generation? How are YOU helping others to find a better future? What type of sun diagram will YOU leave behind?

Acknowledgements

In a book about values and beliefs, it's difficult to pay adequate tribute to all those who have shaped my values and beliefs. Parents Florence and Richard were instrumental in developing the core of who I am. Of particular note, my mother introduced me to formal religion and my father showed me the wonders of nature on countless fishing trips. Helping round out my development as a family team are my brother Mark and sisters Wendy and Elizabeth.

Also making a profound influence on me was Raymond Ingram of Valparaiso, Indiana. Ray was my junior high school science teacher. He showed me that many things around us could be understood in terms of science. Mr. Ingram also showed me that learning one concept can be leveraged to learn the next, more complex concept. I hope I never stop learning.

My loving wife Kathy has taught me community service. As of this writing, she is a 4-H club coordinator for about 100 young people. Her unpaid devotion to the community helps me stay active in the community as well.

Our son Adam has taught me that young people need a careful blend of adult guidance and freedom. At times I found myself trying to make Adam think just like I think. Fortunately, I was able to ease off in time so that a cherished son is still a very good friend.

The final pair who made a profound influence on me, and consequently influenced this book, are Robert J. "Bobby" Keller of Baroda, Michigan and Abraham Lincoln. On February 28, 1980, Bobby Keller suffered a massive heart attack. In spite of our best efforts, Bobby didn't make it. He died in my arms, showing me how fragile, how temporary, life is.

I have read Lincoln's *Gettysburg Address* numerous times. With each reading, I'm moved that its strength is not measured by the count of words; rather its timeless power comes from the choice of a few words which linger in the heart and mind.

Thanks, Bobby. Thank you, Mr. Lincoln.

God's Gifts To Us All

Table Of Contents

Chapter	Title	Page
1	* Tragedy	1
2	* A New Beginning	11
3	* Media Interest	19
4	* An Afternoon At The Resort	27
5	* End Of Day One	37
6	* Prelude	43
7	* Monday Interview	51
8	* The Prediction	61
9	* Why Do You Believe?	69
10	* The Analysis	77
11	* God And Heaven	85
12	* The Departure	93
13	* A World Without Legs	101
14	* A Very Special Person	107
15	* How To Heal	115
16	* What About The Wealthy?	121
17	* A Very Lost Sheep	129
18	* A Day Of Healing	137
19	* The Planning Session	141
20	* Travels Across The Country	147
21	* Preparations	153
22	* *A Day With God* - Performances	157
23	* Adam Speaks	161
24	* And Then . . .	167
25	* And You . . .	171

God's Gifts To Us All

~ Chapter 1 ~

Tragedy

Chapter 1 - Tragedy

The week's vacation at the cabin had almost been ruined by the rains. After three days of continuous downpours, the rain had stopped. There was still a dense cloud cover but this was good enough for Adam Sampson to hit the lake for some bass fishing.

Adam said good-bye to his wife and daughter as he gathered his gear and headed toward the awaiting boat. His wife Susan understood that Adam needed to get out fishing and she was looking forward to taking young Becky to town for some serious Saturday shopping.

The fishing wasn't very good. The rains had turned the water cloudy and Adam couldn't seem to buy a bite. Still, it was good to be out in the fresh air, feel the old motor push the boat and try just about every lure in the tackle box.

Adam had fished until almost dusk and was rounding the point of the lake when he could see flashing lights near his dock. Odd to see lights like that - they looked like police car lights.

As Adam neared the dock, he could see that it was a police car and there seemed to be an officer on the dock waving his arms across the lake toward Adam's boat. The policeman picked up his bullhorn and called out "Mr. Sampson . . . Adam Sampson!"

Adam didn't answer because he could barely hear the officer over the noise of the motor. Adam waved his arm in acknowledgment and pressed on.

The bow of the boat was soon angling toward the dock. The policeman guided the boat safely against the dock. Before Adam could turn off the motor, the officer excitedly reported "Mr. Sampson, I'm Officer Carter. There's been an accident involving your wife and daughter. You need to come with me to the hospital."

In shock from the bad news, Adam awkwardly climbed out of the boat and joined the officer on the dock. "Are they hurt?"

"I can't tell you. I've been instructed to take you to the hospital where you can talk to the doctors."

Chapter 1 - Tragedy

They hurried to the squad car and sped off toward town.

"What can you tell me about the accident?" asked Adam.

"Well, it looks like your wife was driving back from town and going through the cut in the hills leading to the south end of your resort. With all the rains, it seems there was a rock slide. An oncoming car swerved to miss the rocks and forced your car off of the road. The car went down the bank a ways."

"Were they hurt bad then?"

The officer kept his eyes on the road. "I can't tell you."

"Were they killed?" Adam asked with a hushed voice as if he was afraid of the answer he might get.

"Listen, I can't tell you - regulations, you know. We'll be at the hospital in five minutes - just hang on."

It was almost dark as the squad car rounded the turn into the hospital parking lot and pulled up to the entrance with the 'Emergency' sign. Adam got out of the car and dashed in through the large entrance door into the waiting room.

"I'm Adam Sampson and I need to find my wife Susan" Adam announced to a trio of women in white who initially seemed indifferent. "She was in a traffic accident today with our daughter Becky."

"Oh dear" replied the one who seemed to be in charge. "Please come with me."

Adam was lead to a vacant examining room. The nurse said "Please wait here. I'll get Doctor Jeffries."

"Wait!" demanded Adam. "Where is my wife and daughter?"

The nurse squeezed out the door which closed quietly behind her.

After several minutes which hung like hours in the silence of the room, the door swung open. "I'm Doctor Jeffries."

Chapter 1 - Tragedy

"I'm Adam Sampson - where's my wife and daughter?"

"I'm afraid I've got some bad news for you. Your daughter was killed in the accident and your wife is seriously injured." The doctor was calm yet uneasy - he had practiced for 28 years, done this many times, and still each time he informed a family member of a tragedy was as difficult as the one before.

"Dear God!" sighed Adam. His mind became quickly torn between grieving for his daughter and finding out more about his wife. "How's Susan?" asked Adam hoping for some kind of better news.

"Not good, I'm afraid" said the doctor in a rather drawn out manner. "She has severe head injuries and she lost a lot of blood."

"Will she die?" asked Adam with a sigh.

"I can't tell. At times she is stable - at times her vital signs become erratic. If she makes it through the night, her chances get better."

"I'd like to see her - can I?" asked Adam reeling from the burden of almost unbelievable news.

"Of course" replied Dr. Jeffries. "Come with me."

As the two walked down the hallway, Adam's head alternated between watchful looks for his wife and a gaze at the floor in sorrow.

"She's in here" said the doctor as he opened the door toward the operating room. "We need to put on these before we go in" said Jeffries, motioning to the pile of surgical gowns along the wall. "The orderly will help you" said the doctor as he picked up a clipboard and reviewed the current parameters for Susan.

Once dressed, they entered the operating room. There, amidst an array of electronic equipment and hanging containers of various fluids laid a person. There wasn't anything visible that allowed Adam to recognize the patient as his wife. Finally, he edged close enough to see the eyes and mouth which were not bandaged. Yes, this was Susan.

Chapter 1 - Tragedy

"Susan!" said Adam in a voice which would normally have awaked her from a deep sleep.

Susan did not respond.

"Can she hear me?" asked Adam turning to the doctor.

"Maybe. She has gained consciousness from time to time then drifts off. Please be careful of the equipment - but otherwise you're welcome to talk to her or stay by her side" said the doctor in a reassuring manner.

"Susan! Susan, can you hear me? It's Adam - I'm here - I'm here!" said Adam as tears came to his eyes.

This time Susan's lips seemed to move but there wasn't any sound.

"Susan, can you hear me?" asked Adam. "Don't try to talk, save your strength."

"Becky, Becky" whispered Susan slowly.

"I know" said Adam. "It wasn't your fault . . . she's in good hands" offered Adam after a long pause.

"Adam, Adam" whispered Susan, still not opening her eyes. "Love you."

"I love you too!" replied Adam as another wave of tears swept his cheeks. "I love you!"

Again Susan's lips moved without any sounds. The attending machines started to make alarming sounds and lights began flashing.

"Please stand back" ordered Doctor Jeffries as he rushed to Susan's side with the others in the room.

Adam retreated like a fighter getting the knockout punch. The sights and sounds became a blur. Adam found his way to a stool and sat down. A nurse entering the room stood by his side.

"Please take Mr. Sampson outside" ordered the doctor.

Chapter 1 - Tragedy

Adam staggered into the outer room along with the attending nurse. "You can wait here" said the nurse, motioning to a chair.

"What's happening?" asked Adam sheepishly as he slumped into the chair.

"Your wife's vital signs are erratic" replied the nurse. "The doctor and his team are the best we have for this sort of thing."

The minutes passed. A muffled commotion could be heard every once and a while coming from the room. There was really nothing to see. Adam hung his head. He prayed. But there was no prayer that he could think of that sounded like it had enough power to match his level of mental anguish. And yet he prayed some more.

Eventually the door to the operating room opened. Doctor Jeffries emerged and removed his surgical mask. He looked at the eyes of the nurse who was with Adam. In a split second, their eye contact spoke a message that each knew from their years together.

"I'm sorry, Mr. Sampson. There was nothing we could do" offered Doctor Jeffries and he placed a hand on Adam's shoulder.

"No! Dear God no! - Susan!" cried Adam as all that was dear to him in life had been lost in a single day.

"Someone! Please help me!" demanded Adam.

The others in the room looked at each other, knowing that there were no words for situations like this. The nurse attending Adam put her arm around him. This seemed to be the best help that anyone could have offered.

After some time, Adam was lead to another room. Things were still a blur. His stomach ached with a pain he had never felt before. He signed some papers and sipped some coffee.

Eventually he found himself in the emergency room waiting area. Officer Carter was waiting there. "I'm sorry to hear how things turned out Mr. Sampson. I'll be

Chapter 1 - Tragedy

glad to take you back to your cabin at the resort or take you over to the town's car rental if you think you can drive."

"I think I'd like to get my own car" said Adam. "I'll take it easy - I'll stop if I need to."

Adam was about to leave the emergency area, when he stopped by the outside door and turned around. Standing back at the admissions counter were Doctor Jeffries and most of his team.

Adam walked back and shook the doctor's hand. "Thanks for keeping her alive until I could get here. It meant a lot to me to have a chance to say 'Good-bye'" Adam started crying again. The senior nurse shed some tears in response.

"I'm not sure that WE kept her alive" replied Jeffries. "I think that Susan had the most to do with it - she hung in there until she could say 'Good-bye' to you."

"Thanks anyway" sobbed Adam as he turned and left with the officer.

Soon Adam signed for a rental car and carefully drove back to the resort. He took the route which went through the cut south of the resort. He wanted to see the scene of the accident.

It was about 1 a.m. and a new storm seemed to be building. Adam's mind raced with thousands of bits of thoughts - nothing seemed to be a complete idea - some memories of the old days - some glimpses of Becky's birth - their wedding day - the scenes of the hospital.

The headlights rounded the curve at the cut. There, next to the hill were many of the rocks which had been washed onto the road. They had been moved off to the side, but the headlights picked up portions of skid marks and the shimmer of small shards of broken glass. On the right, a path of crushed bushes and small trees marked the spot where their car had gone over the edge. As a back road in a rural area, this section of road wasn't protected by a guard rail.

Adam pulled the rental car into the scenic turnout 100 yards beyond the accident scene. He could see the lights from the resort down the road. Susan and Becky had come so close - and yet they were gone forever.

Chapter 1 - Tragedy

Adam got out of the car and looked out across the valley below. Susan had always liked this area and especially this view. Only a few lights could be seen in the valley below due to the remoteness. Thunder rumbled in the distance.

As Adam stood next to the car, a raindrop hit his cheek. Then another. Adam suddenly associated the rain with his sorrow. It was the rain that caused the rock slide. It was the rain that claimed his Becky. It was the rain that had taken his beloved Susan from him.

Adam threw his arms skyward and shouted to the clouds a primeval scream which contained his sorrows, his anguish, his despair. "Aaaarrrrrrrrrgggggghhhhhhhhhh........." It was no word at all and yet it would be understood by people of any language.

Instantly, the sky answered Adam's cry. The rapier thin lightning bolt raced from the far reaches of the heavens and seemed to stop just above Adam's head. A ball of plasma formed and subdivided into tendrils of electricity which enveloped him. His body shook violently as the charged particles controlled his muscles. His knees gave way as he slumped to the ground. The ball of charged particles seemed to cover him like a blanket. The rain started falling harder as Adam fell the remaining distance to the ground.

As his chin came to rest at the edge of a mud puddle, his tormented mind was erased of all the painful thoughts. Adam slept.

The rain continued for the next two hours.

**God's
Gifts
To
Us All**

~ Chapter 2 ~

A New Beginning

Chapter 2 - A New Beginning

It was just after daybreak. The rain had stopped but the thick clouds remained. Everything was wet from the rain of the night before. Colors were varying shades of gray.

Adam was on the ground where he fell during the storm. His clothes were soaked, muddy, and a bit singed from the lightning. He started to move but every part of his body hurt. He moaned in response.

Although he had not opened his eyes yet or lifted his head, he thought he could hear singing. Yes, there were definitely the sounds of many voices off in the distance.

Adam fought back the pains of his aching body and sat up. At the same time he managed to open his eyes slightly as if the morning's dim light was too bright. His head felt like a swarm of bees were stinging from the inside. He was wet, sitting next to a car he didn't recognize, and he was outside. He struggled to remember how he had come to this place. He could summon no answers. Still there was this singing again which seemed to be calling him.

As he stood up, Adam lost his balance, staggered to the car and rested his elbows on the hood. He remained there for a moment and tried to look around. The singing had stopped. He struggled to clear his head and remember who he was or where he should go. No luck.

Suddenly the singing started again. It was coming from the direction of the resort by the lake. Adam decided to go and have a closer look.

Adam tried to walk from the car, but his legs were weak and his balance was erratic. He went from tree to tree along the road, using each tree as a crutch to keep him from falling.

Eventually, Adam could see some people assembled on the beach of the resort. They weren't singing now, but nobody else was out at that time of day. Adam paused to watch from the base of a tall pine. The group was mostly teenagers and there was one adult. They were all wearing white robes.

As Adam watched, the adult walked out in the water and began talking to the young people. Adam couldn't hear the words, and moved a couple trees closer.

Chapter 2 - A New Beginning

Adam could hear a word every now and then, but nothing made much sense. Then one of the teenagers waded out to the adult. The adult said some more words and then took a double handful of water and dropped it on the head of the young girl. The adult said some more words and the girl returned to the beach. There the others seemed to congratulate her and Adam could now see some adults were sitting on picnic tabes just off the beach. The girl walked over to one of the tables and grabbed a towel as a second girl waded out in the water to the adult. One of the adults at the tables had a camcorder and was recording the proceedings.

For reasons Adam couldn't understand, he was drawn to the proceedings. Soon he found himself at the water's edge.

"Who's the derelict?" asked one of the boys from the group of teenagers who had yet to make the trip into the water.

Adam paused for a moment. The word 'derelict' was one that seemed strange being used to describe him, but as he slowly examined his clothes, he could see they were a muddy mess. He reached for his chin and removed a clump of mud from his neatly trimmed beard. No, this didn't seem right - and yet it didn't seem to matter, either. Adam waded out in the water just as a third girl was completing her ceremony.

"Sir, these proceedings are not open to the public" said the young man who had just sent the girl to the beach.

"I have come - please give me life" said Adam although he wasn't sure what his words meant or where they came from.

"I'm sorry, sir" replied the pastor, "but this is part of my church's baptism class."

Adam looked the pastor directly in the eye and said "I come as a child of God. I need to be born again."

As the pastor pondered the moment, the last girl who had remained nearby began tugging at the sleeve of the pastor's robe.

Chapter 2 - A New Beginning

"Father Kanger, that's Mr. Sampson - I heard his wife and daughter were killed in that wreck yesterday" whispered the young girl to the pastor. "Why not do as he asks?"

"I see - very well" whispered the pastor as the girl stepped away.

"Mr. Sampson?" said the pastor - half as an address and half as a question to confirm the identity of the man.

"Yes" replied Adam as he stood in front of the pastor.

"What religion are you?" asked the pastor, hoping to be able to provide some appropriate words as he had studied all religions extensively.

"I don't know" answered Adam, somewhat in surprise that he couldn't provide a good answer to what sounded like such a simple question.

The pastor decided to keep it plain and simple since Adam didn't seem to have the ability to reason. "Do you believe in God with all your heart and with all your soul and with all your mind?"

"I do" replied Adam.

"Do you confess your sins of this life and hereby swear to sin no more?"

"I do" replied Adam as his head dropped to look down where the pastor was gathering handfuls of water.

The pastor dumped the double handful of water on Adam's head. The teenagers ashore watched in amusement to see what would happen next.

"Your sins are forgiven" proclaimed the pastor. Remembering Adam's initial request, the pastor added "You are now born again. Go and sin no more! May God be with you always."

Adam stood motionless for a moment, his eyes still staring at the water's surface. Drops of water dripped from his hair and his beard.

Chapter 2 - A New Beginning

Suddenly, a beam of light pierced the gray morning sky. Surely this was a sunbeam, but never was one so bright, so focused, so pure. The beam struck Adam in the middle of his forehead. Adam was aware of the warmth and brightness and lifted his gaze from the water's surface and looked to the source of the light.

In the meantime, the pastor had taken a step backwards "Dear God" he gasped.

The group on the beach became silent. The adults at the tables stood up to see better.

A smile came to Adam's face. The beam of light grew to cover his entire face and then covered his upper body. Adam raised his arms to the heavens with his palms upward as if to catch all of the light that was falling upon him. From the beach, it looked as if the beam was charging Adam's body as he inhaled deeper with each breath. The glow from the beam illuminated the area and yet continued to be focused only on Adam.

The beam then faded. Adam turned to the beach. The small crowd stood dumbfounded. The pastor and the girl remained in the water.

"Rejoice!" proclaimed Adam. "Today God is alive in me and I will share the words of God with all the people."

Adam then turned his back to the beach and faced the open waters of the resort.

"Behold, the smiling face of God!" said Adam as he stretched his arms upward.

The cloud cover began to churn. Gradually, the clouds above the resort began to thin. The day began to brighten as the local clouds dissipated. Soon there were blue skies and bright sunshine - but only over the resort and the nearby lake. The grays of the cloudy morning gave way to vivid colors.

Adam turned back to the beach. Most of the morning's gathering were on their knees, feeling the warmth of the emergent bright sun and overpowered by the proceedings.

"No cloud will cover this place for seven days" stated Adam.

Chapter 2 - A New Beginning

Adam then placed his hand on the pastor's shoulder. The pastor's mouth hung open in amazement. "Go now and spread the good word - God is alive - God is here - God is with me - I have come to share God's words."

Adam waded to the shore, smiled at the teenagers and the adults, then walked to his cabin. He was bursting with energy and power - and yet he knew he must wait.

At the beach, the pastor returned to shore and the adults came over and discussed what they had just seen. There were parts they all remembered the same but they politely argued about the exact words which were spoken. One of the adults suggested the whole thing was mass hysteria, but the others pointed to the opening in the sky. It looked like the eye of a hurricane as it was clear that there were dense clouds in every direction.

Ted Berhman informed the group that he had recorded the activities on his camcorder. He was recording the baptism and just kept rolling when this stranger walked into the middle of things. The group went over to one of the cabins that had a VCR and examined the tape. Although they couldn't understand all the words being spoken, the images were unmistakable. Adam wading out to the pastor, the initial beam of light, Adam raising his hands to the light, Adam turning to the beach after the beam faded, Adam saying some words to the people at the beach, then facing the waters and raising his arms as the clouds cleared.

They argued about whether they should call the police but decided no crime was committed. Eventually, Ted offered to drive the 30 miles to the nearest TV station and show them the videotape. The group agreed that was the best thing to do. The pastor agreed to go along once he changed his clothes.

**God's
Gifts
To
Us All**

~ Chapter 3 ~

Media Interest

Chapter 3 - Media Interest

While the pastor changed clothes, Ted Berhman phoned the TV station. He asked for the person in charge and tried to describe the events of the morning. Ted realized as he spoke, he was having a tough time believing his own words. It was not surprising that the people on the phone didn't sound as enthusiastic about the news as Ted was feeling inside. The TV station agreed to meet with Ted and the pastor in about an hour.

Lisa Walters was the news director at the TV station. Normally on a Sunday, she would not be at the station, however, the duty manager called her and told her of Ted's story. Even that may have been dismissed, but the fact that a pastor was involved made this story sound somehow different.

Ted and the pastor arrived in separate cars but had followed each other from the resort. Ted carried the videotape from the car to the front door of the studio with a tight grip - he knew he had recorded something valuable - he would allow nothing to take it from him.

Lisa was waiting inside the lobby of the building. "Hello. I'm Lisa Walters, the news director here."

"Hi. I'm Ted Berhman and this is Reverend Kanger."

"I understand you two have something exciting captured on videotape" queried Lisa.

"Yes, it's quite remarkable" said the pastor. "I have never experienced anything quite like it."

"Please come with me to one of our editing workrooms and we'll have a look at the tape" said Lisa as she motioned toward one of the hallways. "If you don't mind, I'm going to break the tab on your tape to protect it from being recorded over - it's a good precaution to take. If you want to erase it later, you can place some tape over the tab" commented Lisa to the pair who really weren't interested in technical information at the moment.

"You can be sure I don't want to erase THAT tape!" exclaimed Ted.

Chapter 3 - Media Interest

"Well, let's have a look" commented Lisa as she dropped the tape into one of the machines.

The tape started with the group together on the beach singing some hymns. "You can skip over this" said Ted. "Mr. Sampson will appear in the lower right corner of the screen in about 30 minutes."

Lisa deftly operated the controls of the machine which made the scenes flash by in fast speed.

"There! Right there!" shouted Ted as the section of the tape came up where Adam Sampson came on the screen. "I thought he might be going to hurt the kids, so I kept rolling."

Lisa set the machine for normal speed and turned the sound up. She watched intently as Ted and the pastor narrated the images they were seeing. "Wow! Amazing!" remarked Lisa from time to time. She had seen countless hours of video in her career. This one was indeed special. They watched it twice at normal speed and once in slow motion.

"I don't see any trickery" remarked Lisa as she studied the slow motion frames intently. "You'd be surprised what some people put together with their camcorders. We always have to be careful of these hoaxes."

"I can assure you this is genuine!" replied the pastor somewhat defiantly. "It's exactly what happened!"

"Please don't feel like I'm accusing you of anything. It's just in my business, it pays to be a little skeptical."

"You have a steady camera hand, Mr. Berhman" complimented Lisa. "The video from most amateurs is quite shaky."

"I used to be like that too" replied Ted. "I've been shooting for five years and know how important a steady camera is. I was seated at a picnic table and was resting my elbows on the tabletop. I think that helped a lot."

Chapter 3 - Media Interest

"Would you two mind making some statements on camera about what you saw?" asked Lisa as she wrote some notes.

The two looked at each other. They knew they were coming to a TV station, but the duo only thought about showing the tape and explaining. The idea of being on camera took them by surprise.

"Well, I don't know . . . " stammered Ted. "Some of my friends might not take all of this quite the right way."

"I believe I witnessed some form of act of God" said Pastor Kanger after thinking about what Ted had just said. "My job is to spread God's word - and that is what Mr. Sampson asked me to do. Yes, I'd be glad to say some words about what happened."

Lisa picked up a phone and made a couple of calls. Ted and the pastor looked at each other and smiled. They had worried that nobody would believe the story they would tell but Lisa seemed to have accepted everything they had to say. "Reverend Kanger, I'd like to have you step over to one of our studios and I'll ask you some simple questions. We'll piece together sections of it for broadcast."

"Sounds good to me" replied the pastor. Lisa made it sound so easy. He had been in TV stations before to record public service announcements for his church, but this time he didn't have a prepared script or an outline.

The taping went as Lisa predicted - real smooth. The pastor answered Lisa's questions in a calm, natural manner and Lisa made some introductory remarks and some closing remarks. She also recorded a 'teaser' where she just asked "What happened up at Long Lake today? Tune in and watch the six o'clock news for the full story." She told her assistants to mix it with some of the video and get the teaser on the air.

"So what's next?" asked Ted.

"Go to the scene" reported Lisa. "I've had some people come in to form a mobile team and they are getting one of our vans ready to go out to the lake. Are you two coming along?"

Chapter 3 - Media Interest

"Not me" said Ted in a rather apologetic manner. "I've got a house full of people coming over to my place this afternoon for my daughter's baptism party. My wife would clobber me if I didn't show up."

"No problem" said Lisa as she handed Ted's videotape back to him. "I had a copy made while we were taping our studio shots. Something real special there Mr. Berhman."

"How about you, pastor? Care to join us?" asked Lisa as she was gathering some things from her desk.

"Yes, I think I will join you" replied the pastor. "The ceremony at the lake was my service for today, I'm single and was only planning to visit the various open houses of the participating families for the rest of the day. I'm not sure what really happened at the lake this morning, but I feel I can't rest until I know more."

"Great!" said Lisa as she picked up the phone and made a couple more short calls. "Are you riding in the van with us or driving yourself?"

"I think I'll just follow you in my car" replied the pastor.

"See you in the lot in five minutes" replied Lisa as she was now barking out commands to some of the people who appeared to have just arrived at the studio.

The ride to the resort was uneventful. The TV van pulled in the parking lot which looked down at the beach. The pastor parked next to the van.

The pastor sprang from his car just as Lisa and her crew climbed out of the van.

"Did you notice the sky?" asked the pastor, grateful to see that things were just as he had left them - dark clouds everywhere but a large clear area in the sky above the resort and lake. The midday sunshine seemed especially bright.

Lisa and her crew were standing together near their van. All had their hands on their hips as they stared at the sky in amazement.

"This is supposed to stay like this for seven days?" asked Lisa, still not sure what to make of the sky.

Chapter 3 - Media Interest

"That's what I thought he said" answered the pastor. "But I would sure like to talk to him again."

"Let me tell you a few things about our Mr. Sampson" said Lisa as if she was a detective who had just broken a tough case. "His full name is Adam Douglas Sampson. He sells real estate in town. He has leased his cabin here for the last three years."

"You people are good!" exclaimed the pastor. "How did you find out so much?"

"Guys, take some shots of the sky and the general area" Lisa said to her crew. "I had a couple of my people make some calls. One started calling the Sampsons in the phone book and asking if they were the ones with the cabin at Long Lake. We got a hold of someone who had gotten some of Mr. Sampson's mail once by mistake and knew he lived on the north side of town - in the subdivision by the golf course. Another call to the manager of the Long Lake Resort confirmed it was Adam Sampson and the information about the lease. We called the police and confirmed that it was his wife and daughter that were killed yesterday in the wreck south of the lake."

"You certainly are thorough!" commented the pastor as he shook his head "And fast!"

"Have to be in this business" replied Lisa as she organized material in a small notebook. "If you take your time, most stories will get away - or another station will beat you on the air. If you don't check out a few facts, you can end up looking pretty foolish - besides, these checks often provide information which can bring a different angle on a story."

"Well Mr. Kanger, let's got to cabin number 5 and see what our Mr. Sampson has to say. Come on guys!" Lisa shouted to her crew who had wandered down to the beach. "I want rolling video when Mr. Sampson answers the door."

**God's
Gifts
To
Us All**

~ Chapter 4 ~

An Afternoon At The Resort

Chapter 4 - An Afternoon At The Resort

Adam spent the rest of the morning getting cleaned up and looking at the things in his cabin. He knew this was his cabin, yet the contents seemed to belong to someone else. He looked through his wallet at the driver's license, the credit cards, and all of the other things tucked away. Most of the contents were still wet from the rain the night before and his walk in the lake earlier that morning.

Adam laid everything out so it would dry. Even the money looked strange to Adam. He picked up a few of the bills and examined them carefully as if they were some foreign currency.

Adam felt especially strange as he handled the items belonging to Susan and Becky. He felt no remorse, but had a feeling of longing for some good friends.

As he cleaned up, Adam stood for a long time looking in the mirror. The image staring back at him looked distant, strange, even a bit out of focus. It didn't really seem to be him and yet it followed his every move.

Adam knew he would be having guests before the end of the day, but not sure who they would be or what he would say. He sat with his feet stretched out on the couch. He watched through the window as small groups would walk down to the beach, an adult or sometimes one of the children from the morning would point to different places and seemed to be acting out the morning's events. Most of these groups would ultimately end with the person pointing to Adam's cabin, and in seeing him look out from his window, the group would then quickly disappear.

There was a knock at the door. Adam's confusion disappeared as he got up to answer the door. In an instant his mind was clear, focused, and his energy from the morning was with him again. His mission was about to take its next step.

"Mr. Adam Sampson? I'm Lisa Walters from TV23. Would you mind answering some questions about what happened at the lake today?"

"Of course not. Please come in" said Adam as he gestured to Lisa, her crew and the pastor. As Adam closed the door, he noticed a group of people had gathered near the TV van and were curiously watching to see what would happen.

Chapter 4 - An Afternoon At The Resort

"Mr. Sampson, I'm Arthur Kanger. I was in charge of the baptism this morning" said the pastor. The cameraman moved to frame the scene as Lisa kept the microphone near the two without blocking the camera view with her body. Adam and the pastor shook hands.

"Pleased to meet you formally. I hope I didn't give you too much of a start this morning" Adam answered.

The pastor continued as if the camera crew wasn't present "I was a bit surprised . . . and would like to better understand what it all means."

"And so would our viewers" inserted Lisa as she saw an opportunity to gain control of the interview.

"Basically, I have been sent by God to be a messenger" replied Adam rather matter of factly. "In the storm last night, my mind and body were prepared for the work to be done. This morning, with Pastor Kanger's help, I received the blessing of God's vision and was given God's word. The clouds were parted as a sign of God's power and to show the truth of my words. The opening in the clouds will be there for seven days for anyone to inspect or study."

"Mr. Sampson, is it true that your wife and daughter were killed in a traffic accident yesterday?" asked Lisa carefully, watching for the reaction on Adam's face.

"Yes" replied Adam calmly.

"Don't you morn their deaths?" asked Lisa, surprised that her earlier question hadn't received a more profound response or a more visible reaction.

"No" replied Adam, again without much feeling. Looking directly into Lisa's eyes Adam continued "They took their place with God. Now God is with me. They are with me. One day I will join them."

"Are you claiming to be a Christ?" asked the pastor, who had suddenly become skeptical hearing Adam's latest words.

"I don't think I understand the question" replied Adam innocently.

Chapter 4 - An Afternoon At The Resort

Lisa jumped in "You claim to have been given God's word but you are not the son of God? Are you a Moses or a prophet or something?"

Adam replied calmly "I'm not familiar with your references. I know that I, like all of you, am a child of God. I know I have been instructed to give God's word to the people of the world."

Lisa was quick to challenge Adam's latest claim "Our sources say you sell real estate back in the city. What do you have to say about that?"

"That WAS true" replied Adam. "I don't do that anymore. Today my life has a different purpose."

The pastor and Lisa looked at each other, each hoping the other would come up with the next question. Finally the pastor took the lead "What exactly is the 'Word' that you say God has instructed you to give to His children?"

"There will be specifics in the weeks to come, but generally, God wants all people to know God is alive in each of them. God wants to show them God's way, show them they have the ability to make the world a better place, and to stop the destruction of God's creations."

"Which religion do you claim to represent?" asked Lisa.

"I am of no religion, but of all religions" replied Adam quickly.

"What do you mean by that?" asked Lisa, trying to ponder the deep meaning of Adam's words.

"I am led by God's word. God's words are for everyone. It doesn't matter what religion someone claims - God claims all people."

"What would you have me do?" asked the pastor, now torn between declaring this person an imposter or giving Adam his undivided energies.

"Get this interview on TV . . . spread the word about what you have seen. Come back tomorrow. You'll think of many more questions by then."

Chapter 4 - An Afternoon At The Resort

Lisa had a surprised look on her face. Adam had taken control of the interview; she knew that wasn't supposed to happen.

"You'd better be going or you won't make the six o'clock news" warned Adam.

"Oh, yes. You're right" said Lisa as she looked at her watch. "Let's shoot a close outside."

Lisa thanked Adam then lead the crew and the pastor outside. Adam looked at the crowd by the parking lot. Most turned aside to avoid Adam's gaze. Adam smiled and went back inside his cabin.

"If you don't mind, I'd like to hang around?" asked the pastor.

"Not at all" responded Adam. "I'd like to have the company."

The TV crew loaded their van and was on their way. Most of the crowd dispersed while others continued to debate the day's happenings.

"Your heart seems to be full of questions you're afraid to ask" commented Adam as he reacted to the pastor's awkward looks around the inside of the cabin.

"You're right, of course" said the pastor as if he had been caught doing something wrong. "I'm not really sure how to start."

"Why don't we go for a walk around the nature trail that goes along the lake?" suggested Adam, hoping to put the pastor at ease.

"Sounds good" replied the pastor. "Now that it's such a beautiful day, we should take advantage of it - right?" As the pastor looked up at Adam, he felt himself grinning at his own comments - they had sounded more sarcastic than he intended.

Adam returned the pastor's grin with a smile of his own. "Come on, we have much to talk about" offered Adam as he opened the cabin door and headed to the nature trail.

Chapter 4 - An Afternoon At The Resort

"You would probably feel more at ease if we got to know each other better. Why not tell me something about yourself?" suggested Adam as the two walked slowly down the wide path.

The surface of the lake was still. The far side of the lake and the sky were mirrored in the surface between the patches of aquatic weeds. All of the colors were deep and rich. The scene had the qualities of the finest postcards of the area. As the two walked, they were flanked by the lake on their right and the sounds and smells of the pine woods on their left. In the distance were the dark clouds. The threatening clouds were keeping people near their cabins, leaving the lake deserted in the middle of the afternoon. Adam and the pastor pressed on.

"Well, let's see" started the pastor, trying to decide on the level of detail for his life's story. "I grew up in the southern part of the state. There, I went to college and studied theology. After graduation, I traveled for a couple of years, trying to decide what I wanted to do with my life. I sent out some letters and got an invitation to be the assistant pastor at the church east of here. I accepted, wanting to know if I wanted to devote my life to preaching, or if I should look elsewhere for a profession. I've been here for about a year and a half."

"Have you arrived at any conclusions?" asked Adam, pausing to pick up a pine cone.

The pastor was finally starting to feel at ease. He felt like he was talking to an old friend.

"Nothing definite. Right now - at least until today - I've had mixed feelings. Our congregation is small, so I know just about everyone by name. I like that part - and this morning - yeah, that's a good example. In our baptism ceremony, for some of the kids, it's a very moving experience. It's a great feeling to be part of such a powerful experience in their lives. But for some of the kids, I know they are just going through the motions - and, I'm embarrassed to say, I'm not as enthusiastic with them - so I tend to just go through the motions as well. There's a lot our church could do, but with the small congregation, there's not much money to operate with. Sometimes, I can't imagine doing anything else - sometimes, I wonder what I'm doing here."

Chapter 4 - An Afternoon At The Resort

"Interesting" responded Adam, taking a seat on a group of rocks in a clearing by the water's edge. "Has today changed your feelings?"

"I'm not sure. It's as if there is some unstated question about my life's purpose - I still don't know the answer, but I have the feeling that you can help me find the answer" replied the pastor as he stood by the rocks at the shore. When he spoke, he gazed across the lake, as if looking for his answer out there.

"What would you say is the purpose of your life?" asked Adam.

"I guess it really has no defined purpose" replied the pastor, taking a seat on a rock by Adam.

"And this is your problem - but don't feel alone, it is also one of the problems of the world. A few people stand for good, a few stand for evil, - most stand for nothing. God wants all people to have purpose in their lives - to make the world a better place - to care for each other - to care for the planet, the air, the wildlife, the water. Life is a most precious thing. Too many of God's children are doing nothing with it. Too many are doing bad things with it."

Adam stood up and placed his hand on the pastor's shoulder. "When you give all of yourself to a purpose - and give without reservation - every day of your life - and expect nothing in return for your efforts - you will find the answer to your question. Today, you lack purpose. Today, you are giving only some of the time. The inconsistency is the source of your confusion. Come, let's walk some more" said Adam, leaving the pine cone on the rock.

As the two followed the path, they walked more than talked. Finally, the pastor decided to pin Adam down a bit. "When you said you are carrying God's message, does God speak to you, like we are talking now?" asked the pastor sheepishly, not wanting to offend Adam.

"No. It's hard to explain. My mind is filled with visions, some of the past but many of what is yet to come. At times when I think I'm about to have a question about it all, the answer suddenly is in my mind before I can collect the complete question. Other times, like during the interview earlier this afternoon, I know God will give me the right words at the right times."

Chapter 4 - An Afternoon At The Resort

Adam paused and took a deep breath. "I love the smell of the pines! It's amazing, when you look at things carefully, how God's work is so intricate, so complex, so designed to stimulate all of our senses. It's sad to see people pass by and not appreciate it - sadder still to see people abuse it."

"Is that one of God's messages?" asked the pastor, behaving a bit like a student with his professor.

"Yes. Of course!" replied Adam as he began walking back toward the cabin. "All God's creations - all are to be cherished, to be used wisely, to be replenished and cared for."

"Come, let's see what they have to say about God on the six o'clock news" offered Adam as they came upon a clearing just off the beach by the cabins.

As the pair walked past the beach, they could see that the parking lot was full. There were groups of adults scattered about. Most were whispering to each other and pointing toward Adam, clumsily trying to hide the fact that they were pointing.

"Looks like SOME kind of word has gotten out" commented Adam, gesturing toward a few of the groups. "They don't know what they're here to see or do - mostly curious."

"I can identify with that feeling" confessed the pastor. This response prompted a definite laugh from Adam.

They walked up the steps to the cabin and went inside.

**God's
Gifts
To
Us All**

~ Chapter 5 ~

End Of Day One

Chapter 5 - End Of Day One

In all her years of broadcasting, Lisa was having more difficulty with the Adam Sampson story than any other she had worked. Should the story be downplayed or should they do a special? What should they say to the home network? If all this was true, Lisa knew her career would really take off if she handled this the right way. On the other hand, if this guy was a crackpot and Lisa treated him with credibility, that could ruin her career.

Back at the cabin, the pastor emerged from the bathroom just as the news was coming on. Adam had already turned on the TV and sat down on the floor nearby.

The Long Lake story was the main news piece. Lisa did all of the narration. Her delivery was one of flatly presenting the facts, with very little opinion. The scenes from the morning's camcorder, Pastor Kanger's studio interview, and the mobile unit's visit to the resort were artfully edited to go along with Lisa's voice. She ended the piece saying that she hoped that it was all indeed a purposeful act of God, for that was something the world could use right now. She also promised to have more on the story tomorrow.

Adam turned off the TV. "Well, pastor, what did you think?" asked Adam.

The pastor felt like this was going to be some sort of trick question and hurriedly thought through all the responses he might make and was trying to select the best response.

"From the heart" interrupted Adam. "Don't tell me what you think I want to hear, but tell me what's in your heart."

The pastor felt guilty, getting caught this way. "I thought it was very good. Ms. Walters presented the facts without distortion . . . it was an accurate report about what happened here and what you said. She treated the issues fairly." The pastor looked up carefully to see if he had said what Adam expected.

"I agree" said Adam.

The pastor breathed a sigh of relief.

Chapter 5 - End Of Day One

"How many of today's news stories are presented with such depth and objectivity?" asked Adam.

The pastor was on the spot for an answer once more and could hardly believe he was starting to evaluate his answers again. Finally he blurted out "Not nearly enough."

"Quite true" responded Adam. "This is another of society's sins in the eyes of God."

"Really!?" remarked the pastor. "I'm surprised that God would be concerned with something as small as the evening news on TV."

"It's much more general than that" explained Adam. "News people are in a position where they have the trust of people - for accurate information. The times they distort the news, they are betraying the trust of man. The same is true of those leading the churches of the world. They have the trust of the people. Many are using this trust for their own purposes - certainly not doing God's work! All those in a position to have the trust of man - media, clergy, politicians, public service groups, medical groups - all need to understand their responsibility - for God has grown tired of many who are betraying this trust!"

For the first time, the pastor was a little frightened. This stern delivery was a side of Adam he had not seen. The pastor coughed slightly and said "You know, I should probably be going."

"As you wish" replied Adam as both rose from their seated positions.

As they walked toward the door Adam continued "You know, pastor, all of God's work isn't sunshine and roses. Much of it is, but sometimes to make the world a better place, you have to do battle with evil and indifference. To be successful, you have to stand strong and often endure great pain."

"I'll remember that" said the pastor, now wanting to stay longer but couldn't since he had talked his way out the door.

"Would you like to stop by tomorrow and talk some more?" asked Adam, sensing the pastor's awkward position.

Chapter 5 - End Of Day One

"Sure! Any special time?"

"Better make it about 8:30 in the morning. The rest of the day will be hectic" predicted Adam.

"8:30 it is" replied the pastor. As he turned toward the parking lot, it suddenly struck the pastor that Adam may have just shared one of his future visions with him. The pastor had been with Adam since the mobile TV crew had left and nobody else had spoken to Adam that afternoon - and yet somehow Adam knew tomorrow would be hectic.

Adam closed the door to the cabin as the pastor drove away from the resort. Just then the phone rang. It was Lisa Walters from the TV station. Adam agreed to a 10am interview the next morning. There would be more equipment and more networks participating in the interview. This was fine with Adam. The next page in God's plan was about to unfold.

**God's
Gifts
To
Us All**

~ Chapter 6 ~

Prelude

Chapter 6 - Prelude

Adam was up early Monday morning. He took a walk down the nature path by the lake in dawn's dim light. The crowds from the day before were not around. Adam found himself at the edge of a clearing at the far end of the pine forest just as the sun was rising from behind the distant hills and penetrating the tops of the rain clouds. Adam leaned back against the last tree and took in nature. The birds of the meadow were singing their finest, although few had begun flying about. Adam savored the sunrise. He knew the day would be filled with people and cameras.

As the sun emerged completely, it was evident that rain was falling elsewhere. The sky remained clear above the lake and resort as Adam had promised. Adam relaxed at several points along the nature trail and enjoyed the sights, sounds, and smells of the early morning.

Back in the direction of the cabins came the distant sound of some large truck engines. The rumble caused Adam to head back down the path toward his cabin. As he made his way to the beach, he could see a large network trailer parked at the far end of the parking lot. There seemed to be two sections of the crew. One group was waving their arms at the nearby scenery, apparently setting up camera angles and lighting. The second group was pulling equipment from compartments on the truck and assembling cables.

The sound of the big truck also brought out some of the others staying at the resort to see what was going on. Adam returned to his cabin and waited.

Adam was napping on the couch when a knock at the door brought him to his feet. As he opened the door, Adam was pleased to see Reverend Kanger, who seemed to have brought an older man along.

"Adam Sampson, I'd like you to meet Winston McDaniels. He's the pastor in charge of our congregation. I'm his assistant. I told him about what happened yesterday and took the liberty of asking him to join me this morning."

Adam shook Winston's hand warmly. "Pleased to meet you. Please come in."

The duo entered the cabin and took their seats on the plain furnishings.

Chapter 6 - Prelude

"Arthur here tells me you have been sent by God to deliver His message to His children" began the elder pastor, almost expecting Adam to say it wasn't true.

"He speaks the truth" replied Adam quickly.

"Why should I believe you?" asked Winston in a quick rebuttal. Arthur Kanger squirmed in his chair, uncomfortable of the courtroom-like proceedings.

"Do you believe in God?" asked Adam, slowing his delivery so that Winston's emotions couldn't build too quickly.

"Of course!" replied Winston.

"Why should I believe you?" asked Adam of the silver-haired pastor. Adam could almost see the pressure rise in Winston. His face was beginning to surpass the crimson of Adam's plaid shirt.

"Mr. McDaniels, it is not my intent to challenge you or play word games. Like your faith in God, which you would struggle to make me believe, my mission is one which I would have trouble making you believe. God has created the clear sky here to show the truth of my words. You did drive through rain, didn't you?" asked Adam, wondering how Winston would explain that.

"We sure did!" exclaimed Arthur. It was as if driving through the rain into the clearing had convinced the young pastor that Adam was genuine.

Again there was a knock at the door. Adam rose to answer it. As Adam walked to the door, Winston made a sour face at Arthur since the old man felt his young assistant was not on his side.

"Good morning, Mr. Sampson. Remember me, Lisa Walters from TV23?"

"Of course" replied Adam. "We're not scheduled until 10, right?"

"Yes, that's right" responded Lisa. "I wanted to make sure you didn't mind if we set up for the interview on your front porch here."

"Whatever you think will work best" answered Adam.

Chapter 6 - Prelude

"You're sure it won't rain?" asked Lisa motioning to the distant clouds and the expensive camera equipment being unloaded from the trucks.

Adam chuckled, then replied positively "It won't rain! You won't even see a cloud overhead."

"Great!" said Lisa. "We'll see you in about 45 minutes." As Adam slowly closed the door, he could see that cables had been snaked from the truck to the bushes at the edge of his yard. Tripods for the cameras were being erected and a second truck was now in the parking lot. Adam could see some cars were having to park on the side of the road.

Adam returned to his seat by the two pastors.

"Please excuse me" offered Adam, "I hope you will be able to stay for the 10am interview."

"We'll see" said Winston, speaking as though he would be deciding for both pastors. Pastor Kanger squirmed a bit at hearing this, but gathered all of his strength to keep from saying something back at his superior.

"Where were we?" asked Adam, folding his hands in his lap.

"You were about to tell us about the mission God has assigned you" said Pastor McDaniels as he used the interruption to change the direction of the conversation.

"God's words are both simple and yet complex" began Adam. "Too many people of the world have forgotten about God. They may attend a religious ceremony once a week, but their actions the rest of the week do not show an understanding of God's word. Too many people in a position to have the trust of men are betraying this trust. People are taking the gifts of God for granted - they are destroying the natural resources - making no provision for future generations."

Pastor McDaniels had assumed the position of *The Thinker*, cradling his chin with his hand. He wanted to ask more questions, but was drawing a blank. After

Chapter 6 - Prelude

some awkward silence, Pastor Kanger asked "What would God want Pastor McDaniels and I to do?"

"Give God's word to your congregation. Challenge them to go out from your church and make a difference in the world. Tell them there will be no sermon next week, but that you will go around the congregation and ask everyone to tell what they had done in the last week to show they were living God's word. There is too much preaching, polite listening, and not enough people living their life as God intended. You've got to get them to think about God in all they think, say, and do. Hold them accountable. Help them develop the habit of LIVING God's way. After some time, they will hold themselves accountable."

"We try our best" replied Pastor McDaniels. "We have youth activities - like the baptism you attended - and we try to get people involved - but sometimes people don't want to participate."

"Those are the people you must reach!" insisted Adam. "Find the ways to stir their hearts and minds. Let them find the joy that a life with God can bring. You know your people - point them in the right direction, hold their hands as they take their first steps, rejoice with them in their accomplishments, and don't let them slide back to their old ways."

Pastor McDaniels sat back in his chair with a sigh. "You certainly have some interesting things to say."

"Mr. McDaniels, you must realize that as a real estate salesman, I could not put together this material - the words you hear come from God."

"Does HE speak to you then?" asked McDaniels as this was an interesting angle to explore - he still wasn't convinced that Adam was who or what he claimed to be.

"Not in words you can hear" replied Adam. "At times it's more like I can see visions - as you might of a movie you just saw - except I see visions of the future. At other times, like now, for some reason I know God will guide my words and actions. I understand better the fact that I know God's word than I understand how I am able to know - and the 'How' is not really important after all anyway, is it? If someone really brings you God's word, is it important how they got it?"

Chapter 6 - Prelude

"I suppose not" replied McDaniels as he raised his eyebrows toward Kanger.

Pastor Kanger smiled. Inside, he was bursting with relief that the conversation seemed to be going quite well, and that he was able to sit quietly during it all. He then turned to Adam and smiled. In his heart, he was certain that Adam spoke the truth. It suddenly hit him that yes, indeed, God's hand did guide Adam's words and actions. Kanger's smile faded as the weight of this realization sank in. He slid to his knees, folded his hands, bowed his head and said "Praise God for His messenger sits before me!"

"Arthur! What are you doing?" demanded McDaniels in disbelief.

"Giving thanks to God - thanks that HE has chosen this time and place - that we may be blessed by being present to see and hear HIS words."

"Don't you think you're carrying all of this a bit too far?" asked McDaniels - things about him were changing too fast.

"Not at all!" replied Pastor Kanger defiantly. "My career is one of service to God." Turning to Adam, he continued "May I join you and help spread the word of God?"

Adam placed his hand on Arthur's shoulder. "I would be honored to have your help. Please, take your seat."

"Arthur!" exclaimed McDaniels "Are you giving up your position with our church?"

"I have just accepted a position with the Church of churches" said Kanger, looking toward Adam.

Adam smiled. There was a knock at the door. It was time for the interview.

**God's
Gifts
To
Us All**

~ Chapter 7 ~

Monday Interview

Chapter 7 - Monday Interview

Adam opened the door to Lisa once more. This time the view out his door looked quite different. The equipment and lights were all set. There were people everywhere. The commotion of the crews getting things ready suddenly stopped as Adam opened the door. There was a strange silence.

"Looks like you have been busy!" exclaimed Adam.

"Yes, we have" replied Lisa. "I'd like you to meet two other correspondents who will be taking part in the interview."

Adam walked out on the porch. The two pastors awkwardly exited the cabin, trying a little too hard to keep from being in the center of the 'stage'.

"John, this is Adam Sampson" said Lisa to a man about the age of Pastor McDaniels. "Adam, I'd like you to meet John Turner, from our parent network."

"Pleased to meet you" said Adam as he extended his hand.

"Likewise" said John coolly as he obviously didn't approve of Adam's casual wardrobe.

"Adam, I'd also like you to meet Denise Esposito. Denise is from the Hispanic station north of here" said Lisa. From Lisa's wrinkled brow, it was evident she caught John's little act, and hadn't shifted her expression to the innocent Denise.

"So pleased to meet you" said Denise as she shook Adam's hand. "I DO hope you're everything you say you are!" Denise tried to look deeply into Adam's eyes as if in there would be the proof she was looking for.

Adam quickly responded by peering deep into Denise's eyes "You have great faith and great hope. You are among the cherished children of God!"

As Denise ended the handshake, her hand dropped rather limply. She took a step backwards as if hit by a sudden blast of air. She was experiencing a feeling she had not known before and asked one of the stage hands for a glass of water.

"Will the pastors be joining us?" asked Lisa as she motioned to the duo who had worked themselves across the porch into a corner by the railing.

Chapter 7 - Monday Interview

"I'd be glad to participate" offered Arthur as he stepped forward.

"How about you, Mr. McDaniels?" asked Lisa.

"I . . . don't know. I've never done anything like this before" stammered the older man.

Arthur tried to calm him down "It's easiest if you forget about the cameras and just talk to everyone naturally."

"Well . . ." Pastor McDaniels was not so much afraid of the cameras as he was unsure how his congregation - and his superiors - might view his participation. On the other hand, if Adam WAS acting on behalf of God, if word got out that Winston had refused to be seen on camera with the man - that wouldn't be very good either " . . . I suppose I'll go along with you."

"Great!" exclaimed Lisa as she directed the crew to wire each of them with microphones and arranged the chairs on the porch into a U-shape.

Lisa got everyone together and gave them a briefing on the format for the interview. She would begin with an overview story, ask Pastor Kanger a few questions, then go to Adam, then to Pastor McDaniels, then invite the other reporters to ask their questions. They would be shooting from three cameras - a stationary frontal and two that would be moving on each side.

As the interview began, the first part sounded a lot like the piece that was on the news the night before. Lisa's interview of Pastor Kanger went smooth and Adam said much the same things he said with the two pastors in the cabin earlier that morning. Lisa turned to Pastor McDaniels. "Pastor McDaniels, what do you make out of all this?"

"I'm not sure what to believe - I mean of course I believe in God" said the elder pastor as he turned to the frontal camera - just to make sure THAT message got on camera - "I'm not sure I believe that Mr. Sampson is a personal agent of God Himself." Winston felt pleased with how he had handled the first question.

Chapter 7 - Monday Interview

Lisa continued "How would YOU explain the videotape of the baptism yesterday or the fact that there are clear skies above us but rain in a hundred miles in every direction?"

"Well, I've seen a lot of surprising things on TV and at the movies - are we seeing some kind of special effects, or an act of God?" McDaniels' sincerity in response came across well on camera. His earlier concerns about being on camera and not looking dignified seemed to fade away.

Lisa turned to her fellow reporters "John Turner from network news, would you like to ask some questions?"

"Yes, thank you Lisa" said John in a stiff, stage-like response. "Mr. Sampson, some would be surprised that a messenger of God would wear a plaid shirt and blue jeans."

"What should I wear?" asked Adam.

"Maybe a suit, white robes - or something a bit more dignified" responded John.

"You need to get beyond the clothes people are wearing or what they might look like - the color of their skin - the way they talk - their customs - look for the good in the heart. The finest clothes cannot conceal the self-serving heart. The dirtiest rags cannot hide the heart that's true to God" responded Adam in a calm even voice.

Lisa turned to Denise Esposito. "Denise Esposito is with us from the Hispanic Network. Denise . . ." said Lisa as she motioned toward Denise. The cameras followed her motions.

"Mr. Sampson, what will you do next?"

"I'll stay here until the end of the week. After that, I'll visit some of the cities and get out to talk to more people."

"Will you come north and attend the churches in our town?"

"No, I'm afraid not" replied Adam. "It may sound strange to you, but God has directed that I enter no church."

Chapter 7 - Monday Interview

"Yes, that is strange - a man of God cannot enter a House Of God?" asked Denise in puzzlement. This was all new for Pastor Kanger who slid to the edge of his chair to hear every word of the answer.

"My mission from God is NOT one of religion - how people express their belief in God. There is no 'right religion' or 'wrong religion'. The rights and wrongs are in how you live your life - what you do with your life - what your life stands for. By not entering any churches, I will make people think about what they are doing outside of their churches. I will play no favorites - take no sides."

"I hope you're not saying churches are bad, are you?" queried Denise in a troubled voice.

"No. The concept of people getting together to praise God, working together to make the world a better place - if your church stands for these things, these things are good. Too many churches are structured around the mechanical motions of worship and fellowship. Throw in some money and a few greedy people - that's the formula for the churches which are only hallow structures - not Houses Of God."

Lisa stepped back in. "Thank you, Denise. John, you look like you have another question."

"Yes I do" said John with a stern expression. "If you're really a messenger of God, why not perform a miracle for us?"

"Mr. Taylor" answered Adam "Isn't the clear sky above a miracle in your eyes?"

"Probably some sort of atmospheric disturbance. Come on. Or don't you really have the power of God?"

"Mr. Taylor, God is much more than magic tricks" replied Adam, seeming to get a bit agitated by Taylor's persistence.

"I don't think you're a person of God at all! I think you're just a smooth talking real estate salesman! You are going to have to do better than some swirling clouds to convince me you and God are on a first name basis!" John straightened his tie, satisfied he had just out-talked a grand imposter.

Chapter 7 - Monday Interview

In the following moments of silence, Adam's look of frustration gave way to a grin, much to the surprise of everyone else in the interview. "Mr. Taylor, you need to be careful what you ask for! You also need to be careful not to mock God!"

"So, what are you going to do about it?" asked John defiantly.

"It is already done" said Adam matter of factly.

"Well, I'm waiting" demanded Taylor.

"Did you have ears when you woke up this morning?" asked Adam with a grin.

John reached for his ears that were now gone. He and the others gasped in horror. John looked on the ground trying to find his ears - there was nothing there - his ears had just vanished.

"Do you believe in God now?" asked in Adam.

"What have you done with my ears?" demanded Taylor. "Give them back to me!"

"God took them, not me" replied Adam. "And God will grow them back in three weeks - but you must start living the life of God."

"But ears don't grow back!" retorted Taylor.

"They will if you believe they will. If you don't believe they can - they won't. It was your lack of faith and your belligerence that cost you your ears. If you have faith, they will grow back. It's up to you."

John feverishly unplugged his microphone and shouted for one of the aides to take him to the hospital.

"The hospital will do you no good" reported Adam. "The only wound is within you. The power to heal is within you as well."

Chapter 7 - Monday Interview

Lisa was shaken by the proceedings, but wanted to keep control of the interview, so she made a 'keep rolling' gesture with her fingers to the crew. "A most surprising turn of events, Mr. Sampson!" remarked Lisa.

"It's important that people understand on a personal level that God is real - that God has the power to make profound changes in their lives - for the better and, as in Mr. Taylor's case, for the worse."

"Denise, do you have any further questions?" asked Lisa of the remaining reporter. From the parking lot came the screech of tires as the stage hand was leaving with John Taylor for the hospital.

"May I touch your hand again?" asked Denise as she knelt on one knee in front of Adam.

"Certainly, but please have a seat" responded Adam in a gentle manner as he took Denise by her hand back to her seat.

As Denise sat down, she began weeping uncontrollably. Pastor McDaniels passed her a clean handkerchief from his inside coat pocket.

Adam then turned to Lisa, "I think it's important to understand that I have no powers and that touching me does nothing. To touch God, open your unselfish heart, and devote your life to living God's way."

"Mr. Sampson, is there a list or a writing which describes the specifics about just what is God's way?" asked Lisa.

"Not that I know of" replied Adam. "If the wise among you would take the best from each of the religions around the world, the words which speak of respect and reverence to God, the words which speak to how people should interact with each other, the words which speak to how people should interact with the natural resources, the words which speak to taking an active part in making the world a better place - both for today and for the future. Live the life of those words and you will find God's way."

"Are you denouncing the Bible then?" asked Lisa.

Chapter 7 - Monday Interview

"No. The Bible contains much of God's way . . . but for today, it's incomplete - or hard to draw the parallels for today's society and technology."

"What about Jesus Christ?" asked McDaniels. "Are people who believe in Jesus wrong?"

"No - you're missing the point. It doesn't matter if you think of God as Jesus, Allah, Muhammad, Buddha, or the Great Spirit Of The Mountain - the important thing is what you do with your belief - what are you doing with your life? The name and the image are not important. You could not draw an accurate picture of God - but God is a part of each of us - and of all things. Anything you might draw and say 'This is what I believe represents God' would not be wrong - but it could not be totally correct either. Don't focus on the differences in religious symbols or mannerisms - focus on the way of life - the implementation of the belief - look for ways to work together for good - for God."

"A belief by itself does nothing. Implementation is everything. There are many who claim NOT to believe in God - and yet they treat one another with respect and dignity - they make the most of the gifts God has made available to them. These 'nonbelievers' are far closer to God than the ones who claim to believe in God but fail to demonstrate they can implement the governing values of their belief. The 'good' who are idle don't do much good at all."

After a pause, Lisa closed "I'd like to thank Adam Sampson for the interview today. I'd also like to thank Pastor McDaniels and Pastor Kanger for their participation. On behalf of Denise Esposito and John Taylor, I'm Lisa Walters for TV23. Stay tuned for further developments in this most surprising story."

Lisa made a 'cut' sign to her crew and ended the interview. Lisa shook Adam's hand and was soon followed by the two pastors. Denise was still quite shaken by the interview and remained seated where she still wept, for reasons she couldn't understand.

Adam sat beside Denise and reached for her hand. "Your tears are filled with joy, aren't they?" asked Adam.

"Mr. Sampson . . . " Denise was having trouble taking deep enough breaths to talk ". . . I feel I'm in the presence of God. It's a moving feeling."

Chapter 7 - Monday Interview

"Miss Esposito, you are always in the presence of God - and have been all your life" said Adam in a reassuring manner. "You will feel better once you have shared your experience with others."

Adam rose and walked from the porch. He talked to a number of the stage hands and shook their hands. He then talked to groups of people who had assembled to watch the interview or had seen the news piece the night before.

The TV crew packed their things and rumbled off in the large trucks. One of the smaller TV vans remained in the parking lot with two workers from Lisa's station. They were assigned to watch for any significant changes.

The news piece aired later that day. The entire interview was shown. One of the side view cameras had caught a closeup of John Taylor's missing ears just before he discovered the fact for himself. This was edited into the sound track for the finished report. Slow motion of the moment when Taylor's ears disappeared were played from all angles. It was so stunning, it almost looked like it was faked. Everyone at the lake knew it was genuine.

The TV station's phone system was swamped after the broadcast. Lisa couldn't remember when there was ever such a response. Most of the people who called didn't really know what to say. Some asked if the story was a hoax or was true. Most just stammered for a few moments, thanked the TV station for airing the story, then hung up.

As evening fell upon the resort, the place was teeming with people. Adam spoke to one gathering around a large campfire. The remote TV crew shot some footage, but nothing exciting happened. Adam retired to his cabin about 10pm. About half of the people dispersed shortly thereafter. The rest got comfortable to spend the night.

**God's
Gifts
To
Us All**

~ Chapter 8 ~

The Prediction

Chapter 8 - The Prediction

Adam and Pastor Kanger stepped out of the cabin about 7:00 Tuesday morning. There were at least 30 people left over from the night before. Some were in the parking lot, going and coming for breakfast. Most of the rest were near the remnants of the large campfire.

A relief TV crew had just taken over for the duo who had the night watch. Adam and the Pastor leaving the cabin caused them to drop their morning papers, grab their gear, and cautiously stalk their prey.

Eight of the picnic tables had been moved near the fire. A few people were still sleeping here and there - some in sleeping bags or covered with blankets - some just stretched out on a bench or on the beach. Adam walked to the largest group near the fire. One of the people there recognized Adam.

"How about a cup of coffee, Mr. Sampson?" asked the man.

"Don't mind if I do" responded Adam with a smile. All the people suddenly became quiet. Most tried to acknowledge Adam with something that was a combination of a bow, a salute, and a wave. All realized the awkwardness of their efforts.

Adam sat down and accepted the cup of coffee which was poured from a large thermos. Everyone gathered around Adam and had a seat on the picnic tables or on the ground. The TV crew split, with one working a camera in the background and the other getting closer with a microphone. They tried their best to blend in with the crowd and not disturb the moment.

"Have you ever considered what all goes into the creation of a simple cup of coffee?" asked Adam, rather rhetorically.

After a short silence one of the children present answered in a shy voice "It comes from coffee beans."

"That's right" said Adam. "A coffee plant must grow and mature. The plant combines the energy from the sun with the nutrients in the ground. Oxygen and carbon dioxide are exchanged in the atmosphere. Growing things like that are among God's great gifts. The beans must be harvested and dried. They are

Chapter 8 - The Prediction

shipped from where they are grown to our country and packaged and distributed to a store."

Adam continued "And how about the water? - the essence of life. It was probably pumped from a well - but where did it come from to reach the well?" Adam looked at the child who had provided the first answer.

"From rain?" answered the child.

"Right" responded Adam. "But for rain, water must evaporate and condense into clouds. The chemical we know as water is an amazing piece of God's work!" Adam paused, then continued "The water we have today is the same water the dinosaurs drank, the water that made up the great ice ages, and rained down upon our ancestors. It will also rain down upon our descendants. Will they enjoy the pure water we have today?"

"And how about the energy to heat the water to make the coffee? It was either electricity or gas. Both of those are energy sources which are mostly derived from things which happened long ago. What will our grandchildren use for energy to heat their water?"

"What happened to the coffee grounds?" queried Adam as he looked around at each of his audience. "They can be used to enrich our soil, but they probably went to a garbage dump somewhere. Even something so simple as a cup of coffee has waste associated with it and so do the processes that make the ground coffee, the transportation systems that move it where it needs to go, and the energy to heat it. People need to understand and carefully manage the wastes they create."

Adam sipped his drink. The crowd sat in silence, reflecting upon Adam's words. Adam finally finished his cup.

"Life is a complex undertaking" pronounced Adam. "As you eat and drink - and live - consider God's great design. Think about everything that has to happen - or may have happened ages ago - in order to support your lives today. Think about future generations. What will they do for food? For drink? For energy? We can be thankful that between God's engineering and our ancestors, we have

Chapter 8 - The Prediction

a chance for survival today. Think about these things and manage our resources and our wastes to give the future a fighting chance for life."

Adam then stood up and handed the empty coffee cup back to its owner and thanked him. He then turned to Pastor Kanger and said "Ready for our walk, Padre?"

"Sure, let's go" replied Arthur.

As the two made their way to the start of the trail, they shook hands with almost all of the people at the gathering. The two from the TV station gestured at each other to decide if they should follow Adam or stay with the van. In the end they decided to call the station, report on what had happened, and get instructions on what to do with the tape they just shot.

Adam and Pastor Kanger walked for several hours. They talked about a wide variety of subjects. From time to time they stopped and sat to better enjoy a particular scene. When they returned to the beach a couple hours later, it looked as if the circus had come to town. The early gathering of 30 was now closer to 300. There were TV and newspaper reporters everywhere. A cluster of microphones had been erected in front of the porch by Adam's cabin in preparation for an impromptu press conference. The noise of a circling TV helicopter added to the terrestrial commotion. Adam released a deep sigh.

A few of the people quickly pointed to Adam and said "There he is!" Adam took the cue and moved toward the stage which was set in front of his cabin.

Members of the press were instantly recognizable. Where the citizens stayed where they were and kept a respectful distance, the press came from everywhere and swarmed Adam, each trying to get in a question and answer before the others had a chance. Adam only said "Hello" or "Good morning" as he made his way to his cabin. He slid a chair from the porch over to the microphone stand and three TV crew hands reacted by coming forward and lowering the cluster of microphones. Adam took a seat and asked Pastor Kanger to bring him a glass of water from the cabin.

Adam began answering questions from the reporters. Most of the questions produced answers he had given before to some other reporter. After about 20

Chapter 8 - The Prediction

minutes, a newspaper reporter asked "Why has God decided that now is the time for Him to chose you as a messenger and relay His message?"

Adam thanked him for the question and said "God has given the word to people many times over history. A few are documented in written history - even more are the subject of legends, songs and folklore in the diverse civilizations around the world. Today, technology has changed. People have the ability to destroy God's creations on a global scale - through sudden acts of aggression and retaliation as well as the much slower poisoning of the planet from wastes. Resources are disappearing. The planet is losing its ability to support life."

"Society has changed - people lack a sense of direction - most are existing but not living - their lives have no purpose - the world is not a better place because they are here. Society's stagnation is encouraged by technology advances where people can waste countless hours . . . listening, watching, playing - not making themselves or the world any better in the process. People saturate their mind with volumes of data, sounds, and images. Too much information . . . too little understanding . . . virtually no practical use of this flood . . . which fills the reservoir of their mind and occupies a significant percentage of their life."

"This technology is not all bad . . . it has brought about media changes. Many of God's words from ages past are lost or mistranslated. The sounds and images you capture today can be experienced first hand, again and again by countless generations. They will know, as you will come to know, that God is real - that God is alive in each of us - that God's gift to us is our lives and our ability to make things better - and that God wants the people of the world to know God's way and make the most out of their lives."

Lisa Walters asked the next question "Mr. Sampson, why doesn't God just use His powers to MAKE the people live their lives His way?"

"God's powers are vast. God can change our weather" commented Adam as he gestured to the blue sky overhead "stop the planets from spinning, or make all of our hearts stop instantly. God cannot control our ability to make decisions. God can provide the consequences - both good and bad - but the ability to make decisions is ours alone."

Chapter 8 - The Prediction

Denise Esposito, who was standing next to Lisa went next "That seems surprising to me, Mr. Sampson. Can you explain why God can't control our decisions?"

"It's both easy and hard" started Adam. "You accept the fact that gravity is an attractive force, not repulsive. Ice formed from freezing water floats on the liquid. These are things you know and accept - you call them the laws of science, laws of nature. What God is and what God can do are really no different. The fact that God 'cares' about all of you and all things is a natural fact - no different than gravity. The fact that God cannot make decisions for you is also a natural fact."

Everyone was buzzing about Adam's last answer. After a few minutes Adam broke the commotion "Before we break up today, you should know about another act of God." The crowd instantly became silent. A faint hum from all the electrical equipment could even be heard. "When the sun comes up tomorrow, a famous blind musician will have his sight restored."

This proclamation started everyone whispering to each other again.

Lisa asked "Can you tell us the musician's name?"

Adam answered "No, but tomorrow you should have no trouble identifying this person."

Adam continued after allowing people a few moments to exchange their picks for the subject of his prediction "Members of the press, I'd suggest you go now and share this news with your readers and viewers. Come back tomorrow and we'll talk some more."

Adam took the glass of water from Pastor Kanger as he rose from his chair. He sipped the water and went over to Lisa Walters and Denise Esposito. He turned first to Denise. "Miss Esposito, you look a bit more composed today!"

Denise reached out and started to shake Adam's hand. "Mr. Sampson, why did you go out on a limb and make such a prediction?"

Adam replied, "They are the words God would have me say. It's the same as all the other words I speak."

Chapter 7 - Monday Interview

Denise was still puzzled, "What if nothing happens?"

"Guess I'll look pretty silly!" answered Adam. "What will happen if it happens exactly like I said though?"

Denise pondered a moment "I imagine people all over the country - all over the world - will start to believe in the things you say."

Adam smiled "Quite a plan, wouldn't you say?"

Lisa entered the conversation "Only if it happens like you predicted."

"Miss Walters, my source of information hasn't failed me yet" answered Adam. "I don't think God will let me down now."

Adam and Pastor Kanger walked around and talked with many of the people who had assembled. Most of the press had scurried off as Adam had suggested. A few walked with Adam and recorded his conversations with the people.

As night fell, another camp fire was lit, followed by a second and a third. There were more than a hundred people preparing to spend the night. The police assigned a couple of units to keep things under control and to keep the access road open. The sudden popularity of the area exceeded the ability of the road to handle the traffic. Adam and the Pastor retired about 10:30. The people around the camp fires talked, sang a few songs, then got quiet as most tried to sleep.

The crickets and frogs in the area seemed to continue the singing throughout the night.

**God's
Gifts
To
Us All**

~ Chapter 9 ~

Why Do You Believe?

Chapter 9 - Why Do You Believe?

Adam was taking his morning shower when Pastor Kanger excitedly knocked on the bathroom door. Adam turned the water off to hear better.

"It's on the morning news! Stevie can see!" The pastor was beside himself with excitement. Adam's reaction was more subdued.

"That's good" replied Adam as he turned the water on once more to finish his shower.

The pastor could hardly wait for Adam to get finished in the bathroom. This was one of those times the pastor's younger age was apparent. His excitement was so intense about WHAT had happened that he didn't consider WHY it had happened.

"Pastor Kanger, you seem surprised that God had the ability to do what I said" commented Adam as he finished getting dressed.

"Oh, it's not that I lack faith in God or in you - but your prediction yesterday seemed beyond MY comprehension - everything else that happened has happened in the area. Stevie was all the way on the east coast - I'm impressed beyond words" said the pastor with a deep exhale and a wave of his arms. He plunked down in one of the chairs to add a final note of exclamation.

"You must remember that it is God making these things happen, not me" replied Adam. "God's powers know no geographical limits. Do you think we'll have much of a crowd today at the news conference?" asked Adam, angling his head to see out through the curtains of the cabin.

"The place is already packed" said the pastor. "I took out the trash earlier and there were people everywhere. Two reporters asked me for some comments as I disposed the trash."

"What did you say?" asked Adam.

"I asked them what THEY were going to do today to make the world a better place" replied the pastor with a sheepish look at Adam to see if he said the right thing.

Chapter 9 - Why Do You Believe?

"You're catching on!" said Adam in an approving voice. "What should WE do today to make the world a better place?"

"Show people the power of God in Stevie's new found eyesight?" said the pastor half as a question.

"Right again" said Adam as it was clear that the pastor's earlier excitement had been displaced by rational thinking.

As the two emerged from the cabin, hundreds of people were there to greet them. Some people applauded, others knelt in reverence. Some media thrust tape recorders and microphones in Adam's face. Adam answered a couple of questions while walking and soon worked his way free to greet many of the people who had gathered. In the end, Adam and Pastor Kanger took off down the nature trail talking with several clergy members, about a dozen media representatives, and about 50 citizens.

As they came upon one of the clearings along the nature trail, Adam took a seat on one of the rocks. The others sat on adjacent rocks, logs, or the meadow which opened next to the trail.

"Members of the clergy" began Adam, "Why do you believe what you believe?"

There was a long silence. Finally a Roman Catholic Priest answered "I find God's words in the Holy Scriptures."

Adam replied "That is the answer to WHAT you believe - or WHERE you find it - but WHY do you believe the Holy Scriptures?"

The priest answered "They have been handed down through the ages as the chosen words of God."

"Are there no recent 'Chosen words of God'?" queried Adam.

"No, nothing official. Are you suggesting the Holy Scriptures are wrong?" asked the priest defiantly.

Adam answered the question with a question. "Is the important thing the book itself or the messages it contains? And if the message is what's important, is the

Chapter 9 - Why Do You Believe?

message about how to worship or how to live? Pretend for a moment that you never saw any of your ancient holy books . . . How would you live? What would you think would be God's way?"

Adam paused for several seconds, then continued "In ancient times - and even today, you argue about points of fact in your ancient manuscripts - whose holy book is holier than someone else's - how God 'favors' one religion or group of people. You kill one another over your differences. This is NOT God's way!" declared Adam with a sudden sternness. "The points of fact in all of your holy books are really irrelevant. Did someone actually do the things which were written of them? However such questions are answered would have no change on how I interact with you, how you interact with each other, what each of us does with our lives. God cares for all things, all people - God has no 'favorites' except perhaps those who live God's way."

"You also argue and kill over 'holy' grounds. The concept of special lands are a creation of man. In God's eyes, all things - all land - is holy and should be treated as such. Man needs to understand this concept quickly and stop the senseless killing and pain around the world." Adam looked at each who were listening with a cold, piercing stare as if to etch his words in their minds.

"Mr. Sampson, you seem to look upon the Bible - our holy books - with contempt. That is hard for us to take" commented the priest as he gestured toward his fellow religious leaders.

Adam replied "There is nothing wrong with your books - only what you are doing with them. If they are a foundation for you to live God's way, then they serve you well. Too many of you, however, are confined by your books, living in the past - trying to find the passages you can interpret which justify your lives of grandeur, twisted to make your people believe they need YOU more than they need God, distorted to justify acts of violence - acts of Godlessness. You may be better off to cast aside your books, take a deep breath of today's air, and begin living God's way to make today and tomorrow - a day which you are proud to have lived. Live each day as if it were your last - as if at the day's end you were accountable to God for all that you did - and didn't do - with that day in your life."

"Do you believe the world is becoming a better place to live? Are the people of the world using the life that God has given them to do good things? Or are they

Chapter 9 - Why Do You Believe?

chasing selfish or self-serving goals? Or just existing instead of living? The ancient writings of the religions of the world are not 'wrong', but we cannot ignore the world around us. There is nothing in any of your documents which describe me or the events which are unfolding around you. You may think you can find passages which suggest these times, but there are none. This is part of God's message to you. You must guard against ignoring the present and the future for the sake of worshiping the past. Also, guard against worshiping the words instead of living what the words mean."

"Look around you." Adam gestured toward the blue sky overhead. "God is trying to get your attention. Show the people you lead how to live the life God has made possible. Get them motivated to make the world a better place. Show them the value of being honest in everything they do and say. Get them to understand the value in helping others. Lead them to see the wonder of God in nature and in natural processes. Open their hearts to the satisfaction of doing the right thing, even if nobody notices. Let them see the potential they have with their life."

The crowd sat in silence, pondering the words they just heard. "Your ancient holy books were written in times very different from today. Many of those who assembled the manuscripts had non-God agendas - to control people - to establish favored positions and titles - to leverage wealth away from people. "

"Ancient people could not comprehend what we understand today - the immense amounts of time for the universe to become what we see today - the vast distances in space - the details of natural forces and physics. Much of what was worshiped in the past is understood today in terms of natural laws and dynamic processes. That does not prove that there is no God, but it does allow us to better understand the world we live in. We have graduated from a world where it was believed God was acting directly to cause what was observed. Today we might attribute to God the fundamental forces of nature and the grand designs behind the processes we have identified. I doubt that your holy books represent the world that we understand today."

"Look to your ancient books as stepping stones. They got you to this point in time - but are they the best you can pass along to future generations?"

Chapter 9 - Why Do You Believe?

"If your books are repositories for the words of God, you need to write what you are hearing right now. What I bring to you and the rest of the world are today's words from God. Listen to them carefully. After you have taken time to understand what God has to say today, think back to your ancient holy books. Many of the ancient writings were attempts to express the same concepts to the people of the day. Find the true words of God in your books. Find the words of man in your books that have been passed along as if they were the words of God. You should be able to see the differences."

"Today is different. The times are different. The people are different. It is time for some new words from God which guide the lives of generations to come."

After a long silence, Adam spoke softly "Come, let's continue our walk."

As the group made their way down the winding nature trail, they were much quieter than before. Most thought as they walked. A few spoke in whispers. They returned to the resort area to what seemed like more people than the land would support. Adam walked up to the cluster of microphones like he did for the past few days and answered more routine questions. At one point Adam became a bit upset when asked "What is the name of your new religion?"

Adam insisted that he represented no religion and that he had nothing to do with the amazing things that people witnessed in the last few days. Adam finished by asking that the people go home and do something to make the world a better place - waiting around the resort could not accomplish that.

About half of the people did what Adam had suggested. The rest hung around to see what would happen next.

**God's
Gifts
To
Us All**

~ Chapter 10 ~

The Analysis

Chapter 10 - The Analysis

Thursday was a non-eventful day. Adam and Pastor Kanger took their walk, attended the 10am interview, and filled the day talking to a host of media and citizens. They retired early that evening and rested for the challenges to come.

Friday morning brought with it a special interview for Adam. He had agreed to undergo a psychological interview by a staff psychologist from one of the major networks. The interview was set in Adam's cabin at 9am and scheduled to last an hour. A single camera recorded the proceedings.

The 10am press briefing was formatted differently. Lisa Walters from the local TV station was scheduled to interview the network psychologist about her interview of Adam.

The group took their place on Adam's porch which was by now a familiar setting for press briefings. Lisa got things started "Doctor, would you share with us your analysis of Adam Sampson?"

"I'd be glad to" replied the doctor. "Mr. Sampson has a complex psychological profile. He has only vague memories of the past and almost no knowledge of any of the major religious books of the world. He is operating under the understanding of a divine assignment. Unlike others I have interviewed, Mr. Sampson's divine assignment doesn't center attention on himself or assign Godlike qualities to himself. Rather his interpretation of his assignment is to get people thinking about God, the gifts from God they have, and to challenge people into making the world a better place."

Lisa countered "Do you think Mr. Sampson is really an agent of God?"

"Well he certainly thinks he is" replied the doctor.

"No, you're missing the point" said Lisa. "Based on your experience, training, and the interview you just completed, do you believe that Adam Sampson is an agent of God?"

There was a long silence while the doctor pondered the aspects of her position. There really hadn't been much time to digest the interview which had just been completed. "Mr. Sampson is an amazing person. I can't ignore the gaps in his memory nor can I ignore the footage I have seen on TV during the week. I have

Chapter 10 - The Analysis

been trained to treat people who are suffering from such delusions, but . . ." There was another long pause as the doctor looked down at the ground. When the doctor looked up, there were tears in her eyes. She turned her head to look at Adam "Yes, I believe Adam Sampson IS an agent of God! There is something so pure about his thoughts and words. He has no hidden agendas. And the events which accompany him defy any explanations which I find valid. For me to arrive at any other conclusion would betray the trust of the network and the viewing audience in my evaluation." The doctor used her fingers to wipe away her unexpected tears.

"Thank you, doctor" replied Lisa, a bit surprised in her formal conclusion. "Mr. Sampson, do you have anything to say about the doctor's evaluation or conclusions?"

Pastor Kanger, who was on the sidelines, let go a great sigh of relief about the doctor's conclusions. Adam, on the other hand, showed no visible reaction to the doctor's evaluation.

"The doctor's last comment was an important one" replied Adam. "The issue is the use of the trust others have in you. As I have said earlier in the week, one of the great abuses of God's gifts is the misuse of the trust of others. It is also important that everyone around the world understands God on a personal level. To get this message across, when the sun rises on Monday morning, all those around the world who are abusing the trust others have placed in them will feel a burning sensation in their right knee. An hour later they will have no feeling in their right leg below the knee. At noon they will experience a burning sensation in their left knee. In another hour, they will lose all feeling in their left leg below the knee. They will be unable to walk. When the sun goes down on Monday, their legs will be good as new."

Lisa took a hard swallow "Just who will this effect?"

"Anyone who abuses the trust of others" answered Adam. "This would include media who distort the truth, religious representatives who are not devoted to God's work, and countless others who are in a position of leadership who are not performing according to what they have told people they can trust. This will also reach individual citizens who misrepresent the truth on personal reports like tax

Chapter 10 - The Analysis

returns and insurance claims and in so doing place a burden on their fellow honest citizens to make up the difference. This is also an abuse of trust."

"Mr. Sampson" countered Lisa in disbelief "For this to happen as you described, it would incapacitate millions - billions of people world wide."

"What you say is unfortunately true" responded Adam. "Each of these billions needs a significant personal event to reshape their value systems. Their wake-up call will be one they cannot ignore or rationalize away. They have control over the decisions they make and how they will make use of their lives. God cannot make decisions for them but God can provide consequences - making their heart stop is as easy as paralyzing their legs."

"Are you suggesting God will kill those who do not change their ways?" asked Lisa who was becoming edgy as she was trying to decide if she would be among the afflicted on Monday.

"God has not provided me with that answer" responded Adam. "I hope it doesn't come to that - there is so much good which could be done!"

With a concerned look, Lisa concluded the interview. People did not come as close to Adam as they had done before. A sense of fear circulated the crowd as each performed a personal assessment. Those who knew they would lose the use of their legs on Monday panicked in an attempt to think of a place where they might hide - only to realize that if what Adam said was true, there would be no place on earth to hide. Many went off by themselves, hanging their heads with great guilt and remorse. Others chose disbelief as a means of coping with the verdict which they had just heard.

Arthur Kanger was finally able to get Adam alone near the beach. "Will I be among the afflicted?" asked Arthur nervously.

"I can't tell" replied Adam. "That's between you and God. I guess one way to look at it . . . " Adam looked out toward the lake as he pondered ". . . either nothing happens - which means you are not betraying the trust of others . . . or your legs are paralyzed for a day - which means you need to change your ways . . . but on the other hand - it means that God is reaching to touch you

Chapter 10 - The Analysis

personally." Adam looked back at the pastor for his reaction to this interpretation.

The pastor struggled to chuckle, as that's what he thought Adam was expecting. It was a most worried-looking effort.

Adam could see the inner torment. "Come friend, let's go for a ride in my boat."

The two gathered a few items and set off from the pier. Adam ran the motor a while, then shut it off and asked the pastor to row.

"I can tell you are still troubled" observed Adam as he gestured toward Arthur's aimless rowing.

"I feel guilty - but not of directly betraying the trust of others - but that there is so much more I could be doing with my life. Too many times I looked for an excuse NOT to do something I knew to be good. If I think long enough I can always find a reason NOT to - but with the same effort, I could be finding ways to be doing good things." Arthur stopped rowing. The boat coasted. The oars floated in the calm water.

"You have made a powerful conclusion" remarked Adam. "What will you do with this realization?"

"Well, for starters . . . " the pastor began rowing again, but in long, slow thoughtful strokes ". . . I'm not going to shy away from people like I used to. I would select people to talk to who I thought would be receptive to what I had to say and avoid anyone who I thought might disagree. I would avoid unpleasant people and unpleasant situations."

"Good" replied Adam as he noticed the pastor was increasing the pace of his strokes and keeping the boat under perfect control.

"I was only finding the sheep that weren't lost" mused the pastor. "It takes extra effort to find the lost sheep, but it's where the greatest good can be done. I need to stop looking for excuses and thinking about rewards for my efforts - I need to be accountable for every day of my life - to live the life God has made possible."

Chapter 10 - The Analysis

"Aren't you still concerned about Monday?" asked Adam of the pastor who was starting to break into a sweat.

"Monday is only one day in my life" responded Arthur. "God willing, there will be many others, each with their own challenges and opportunities. I am prepared to take on life with a new vigor and sense of direction."

"Speaking of direction" added Adam, "shall I start the motor and take us back?"

"If you don't mind, I'd like to row us in" answered the pastor.

The two were back to the dock in about an hour. The people on the shore still had the worried look that Arthur had left in the middle of the lake.

"If you'll excuse me, Adam" offered the pastor "I'm going to take a shower and return to the beach to find some lost sheep."

Adam smiled.

**God's
Gifts
To
Us All**

~ Chapter 11 ~

God And Heaven

Chapter 11 - God And Heaven

With Saturday's dawn came the last clear day for the resort area. Without rain for a week, things had dried out quite a bit. The evening's dew could not provide adequate nourishment for the plants and grasses, especially with the crowds of the week. The people of the resort were looking forward to some rain. Also, Adam had announced that he would be leaving the resort on Sunday. While Adam was very special to the residents, they would not miss the large crowds and media that he attracted.

At the morning press conference, Denise Esposito asked Adam "Mr. Sampson, many of our viewers would like to get a better understanding of God. Can you tell us anything about Him?"

"Yes, of course" replied Adam who began making a number of facial gestures as he gathered his thoughts. He also turned to face Denise in a way that seemed to shut out the other correspondents who were present.

"First of all, it is hard to describe God's true nature and even harder for you to comprehend. I will try to explain things in terms you will be able to understand."

"A good comparison is gravity. The ancients didn't know about gravity, so they made stories to explain it. Today, we understand that gravity is a fundamental force of nature. We don't exactly know how it works, but we know the formulas which describe its effects. We can see evidence of it in action. We fully expect gravity to work in the far corners of the universe much the same as it works here on earth. We believe this same gravity was present in the past and will endure forever."

"God is much like gravity. God is part of all things, in all places, at all times. God can be like a force to cause change - from very subtle details to changes which reach all corners of the universe - the birth and death of stars - the birth and death of man."

"From the Bible we are lead to believe that man was created in God's image" stated Denise. "Is this true?"

"If you mean, 'Does God have two legs, two hands and a flowing white robe?' The answer is 'No'. The way in which man is like God is that we have the ability to understand some complex concepts: right and wrong, stewardship, the

Chapter 11 - God And Heaven

physical laws of nature, the future effects of our actions, to name a few. We can make global changes through our actions. The deer and the butterflies don't have these abilities. We do. So does God."

With a check of her notes, Denise asked "Does God have a name like you and me?"

Adam thought for a moment then responded "It's probably best to stick with the gravity analogy. Gravity doesn't assign itself a name - call itself 'gravity'. When we refer to God, or whatever name we choose, we are assigning a name to the force which governs all forces; the spirit that governs all spirits. To answer your question, the only names for God are those that people have created. Like gravity, God simply IS."

"Are we wrong then to refer to God as a 'Him'?" asked Denise.

"Do you assign a personality to gravity? Assign a gender? You would do better to think of God as you think of gravity - in all places, acting upon us all the time. As we run and jump into the air, we seem to defy gravity for a time. The physicists will tell you this is not true. For a time you can exert a force greater than gravity, but gravity always pulls you back. The same is true with God and man. Since we have the ability to make our own decisions, we have the ability to depart from God's way. God will prevail, you can be sure - it's only a matter of time and place."

"What about Satan? Is there a devil?" asked Denise quietly so as not to offend Adam - or perhaps to avoid being struck down by lightning.

"There is one God" answered Adam. "You have seen God take someone's ears. On Monday, God will paralyze the legs of about half the people on earth. At times even a good father will inflict suffering on his children to teach a lesson. The concept of the devil and Satan were created to allow the ancients to understand the concepts of good and bad and understand which was God's way. Today we have grown to the point where we can better understand gravity. We can now also better understand God."

"Does this mean that there isn't a hell or heaven?" asked Denise in puzzlement.

Chapter 11 - God And Heaven

"If you are referring to a physical place that you can visit - no, there is no place. Heaven and hell are states of mind - states of spirit. Today you have dreams which range from pleasant to scarey. Many of these seem incredibly real. They stir your emotions. Afterlife is much the same. You are in what seems to be a dreamland - it can be a most wonderful experience or the most terrifying you can possibly imagine."

"What about prayer? Does God like it when we pray to Him?" asked Denise.

"God doesn't have 'needs' and therefore doesn't need prayers. At times, it's important that you remind yourself and others that the focus of your life is to God's way. When you pray, if you pray, do it for your own good and the good of those around you - don't do it because you think God likes to hear your voice" responded Adam, this time with a little grin.

Denise continued her questions "Did I hear you say that praying isn't important?"

"Not exactly - let's look at it from a different angle. If you need to pray to keep or regain your focus toward God's way, then by all means - pray. The creatures of the forest and the sea focus primarily on themselves and on the 'now'. Man has this tendency also. For many, prayer helps them remember there are other people to consider, other generations to come, the generations gone by - it helps them assess how they are doing with the abilities they have and the challenges they face. Taking the time to consider how you are doing in comparison to what you understand to be God's desires will help keep you close to God. Without these moments, many become selfish, uncaring, self-serving - with little concern for others today or in the future. With these moments of prayer, many can regain their life's focus, find the extra strength they need to meet the challenges of life - perhaps conquering temptations or standing up to peer pressure."

"On the other hand, if you keep God in the forefront of your thoughts every day, you will be living a prayer. Extra words cannot add to your actions. Your every thought and action will be with God's purpose in mind. For such people, a spoken prayer may not be necessary, except when in the presence of others who need some help finding God's way."

Chapter 11 - God And Heaven

"Does God think like you and me? Does God have emotions?" asked Denise as if trying to get to know a new friend better.

"This is the hardest part to explain and understand" answered Adam. Again he took a few moments to gather his thoughts. "There is a consciousness and thinking spirit in God - a wisdom. This 'mind' doesn't ponder options or speculate as we do when we think - it's decisive, straight forward and purposeful. This consciousness doesn't hold all the facts and figures we might associate with a mind, but there is an incredibly complete understanding - almost from an engineering point of view - about the causes and effects of everything everywhere - and the ability to make decisive changes."

"As far as something along the lines of emotions - it would not be the same as we experience, but there are some parallels. There is an intense caring - love if you will - for everything and everyone. There is a sense of satisfaction - not exactly pleasure - when things are performing to their potentials. On the other hand, there is a sense of dissatisfaction when things are not what they should be. There is no fear, hatred, remorse, jealousy, or many of the other emotions we are familiar with."

"There is also an absolute purity - and a vastness in space and time which I cannot adequately describe" continued Adam. "God is everywhere, all the time - like gravity - and yet 'knows' each of us on a personal level."

"I'm a little confused about God 'knowing' each of us personally" remarked Denise as she gestured to herself. "Could you tell us more about that aspect?"

Adam smiled for the moment. "I knew this would be challenging to explain." Adam took a deep breath and continued "God is with each of us." Adam gestured toward the hushed audience. "Each of US is part spirit, part body. God is all spirit and no body. It is through our spirit that God 'knows' us - to a certain extent, our eyes are God's eyes, our ears, God's ears, and our spirit, God's spirit. As each of us know our own hand . . ." Adam held up his hand and looked at it ". . . and we are familiar with it as a part of our body - the feelings of pressure, temperature, pain, and texture it can transmit to our mind - and we know our hand can grip, hold, move - for good and for bad."

Chapter 11 - God And Heaven

"Through our spirits, each of us is a hand of God - a source of information and action and known very well to God. Since we have the ability to make our own decisions, at times we seem to God to be like a hand acting under spasms - not doing what the controlling spirit has intended. When we are living God's way, to God we are like the skillful hand of the master craftsman - able to take raw materials and disorder - and create something good, something of value to the world."

Denise responded "Can God really know each of us as individuals in a world of billions?"

Adam answered "On Monday, only those who have betrayed the trust of their fellow man will be affected. To be selective like that, God MUST know each person as an individual. It may be hard to believe, but you will see on Monday."

Denise then turned the interview over to Lisa who did the formal close for the spot. There was a new hush that had replaced the commotion which usually followed these daily interviews. Adam declined to answer more questions and asked the reporters to take some time to think about what they had just heard. Adam asked Pastor Kanger to do the same as Adam went down the nature trail alone for his walk.

God's
Gifts
To
Us All

~ Chapter 12 ~

The Departure

Chapter 12 - The Departure

It was mid morning on Sunday. Some thin clouds covered the resort for the first time in a week. Adam and the pastor loaded some of their things in the trunk of the pastor's car. One person from the morning's crowd offered to help, which prompted others nearby to do the same. The car was loaded in record time.

Adam walked over to the collection of microphones for a farewell press conference. He turned sideways to address several of the local inhabitants who were standing by their cabins. "Residents of Long Lake Resort, I appreciate the tolerance and friendship you have shown over the years and especially in the last week. This place has been the starting point of something very special for me - I hope you have become equally inspired."

Adam then turned to face the cameras in front. Supplemental lighting had been turned on to brighten the dull colors of the cloudy morning. "Please be careful tomorrow" Adam cautioned. "Many of you will lose the ability to use your legs for the day. Don't engage in any activities where you might endanger yourself. As I have said before, if you will be affected, it will begin as a burning sensation in your right knee. If you start to feel that sensation, your leg will be paralyzed within an hour. Have a plan to get somewhere where you will be safe. Those of you who are not affected, please do what you can to help the others."

Adam continued, "Everyone needs to think beyond the effects they are observing to remember the WHY behind the effects. Those who will lose the use of their legs are in some way betraying the trust of their fellow man. If you are among the affected, look in your heart and you will know where your shortcomings are. Also remember those things that God is bringing to your attention are aspects of your behavior today and in the past - it need not be part of your future if you decide to change your ways."

John Turner, who had lost his ears the Monday before, asked the next question. John was wearing a hat and had the collar on his trench coat in the raised position to hide his disfigurement. "How exactly will this happen as the sun will rise at different times around the world?"

Adam seemed a bit surprised to see John Turner, then smiled warmly. Adam got up from his seat at the microphones and walked slowly over to John. Adam had never done that before in any of his interviews. Adam reached out his hand to shake John's. John reluctantly extended his own hand. Adam took hold of

Chapter 12 - The Departure

John's hand in the handshake position, but only held it. Adam then slowly moved his left hand to cover the back side of John's right. The crowd was hushed in silence as John handed his microphone to a fellow correspondent. John reached his left hand toward Adam's, but stopped short. John then continued by placing his left arm around Adam in a hug. Tears came to John's eyes.

"Mr. Turner, I'm so glad to see you" offered Adam quietly in a reassuring tone. Adam returned to his seat and John used his handkerchief to blow his nose in an effort to compose himself.

"To answer your question, Mr. Turner, it will seem like a wave sweeping the planet from east to west. The far east will be affected first, then Europe and Africa and then the Americas."

John Turner responded "Can someone get on a plane and fly east to west to escape the sunrise to sunset time span where they normally live?"

Adam answered "You cannot run from gravity - you cannot run from yourself - you cannot run from God. Those who try will be affected just as if they had stayed where they were."

With a few more questions, the final press conference at the resort was over. Adam spent a few minutes walking around with Pastor Kanger and greeting people. Some of the people who met Adam responded with reverence, while it was clear others were fearful. Many people treated Adam like a celebrity and asked for his autograph. Adam always declined.

Pastor Kanger and Adam were soon on their way to the nearest large metropolitan area. Pastor Kanger was a little concerned that they had not made hotel reservations before they left. "We won't need to find a place to stay" assured Adam. "There will always be those who will share their homes with us. It might even be some of our friends back there" snickered Adam as he gestured toward the back of the car. Following in parade like fashion were about 50 vehicles. Above was a news helicopter. Everyone was anxious to see where Adam would go next.

Chapter 12 - The Departure

The rural roads eventually gave way to interstates and soon the two approached the city limits. On one of the highway signs was an arrow showing the direction to a city park.

"There, take that exit" directed Adam. "Let's see what is happening at the city park."

As the two reached the parking lot, they were joined almost immediately by both the group following and a new contingent from the city who were listening to broadcasts of the duo's travel from the mobile media.

The first TV news team on the spot had junior correspondent Jeff Gladding. Jeff was eager to get to Adam before any other networks. Jeff wormed his way through the crowd toward Adam with the camera crew close in tow. When Jeff finally got to Adam, a newspaper reporter was there first, but Jeff had the first camera crew. As Jeff waited for an opening to ask a question he looked around nervously for the arrival of other mobile TV units. During a pause, Jeff saw his chance and asked his first question "Mr. Sampson, what do you plan to do in the city?"

Adam responded "Meet some people to start with. I'm Adam Sampson - and you are . . . ?" Adam extended his hand to shake the reporter's hand.

Jeff was surprised by Adam's actions and mechanically responded to shake Adam's hand. Nobody had ever introduced themselves to Jeff during an interview like that. "Uhm . . . I'm Jeff Gladding."

Adam continued, "Well Mr. Gladding, after I meet some people and see some of the city, Pastor Kanger and I will need to find a place to stay. How about if we stay with you?" asked Adam.

"You're welcome to, of course" responded Jeff, rather dumbfound about such a question "but I live in a small apartment on the south side of town. It will be a bit cramped."

"Perfect!" responded Adam in delight. Adam looked at Pastor Kanger who was not showing the same delight Adam found in the situation.

Chapter 12 - The Departure

There was a commotion that seemed to approach Adam. A second TV news team arrived with cameras and lights at the same moment as a number of police officers. The police chief got Adam's attention.

"Mr. Sampson, I'm Police Chief Timms. I want to ensure your safety while you're here in the city."

Adam shook the chief's hand. "I appreciate your offer, but there is no need for concern."

"Our city, like any large city, is not without some isolated problems" responded the chief.

"Chief, slap my face" instructed Adam.

"What!?" asked the chief in disbelief.

"Go ahead" said Adam. "It's ok - just try."

"All right" said the chief reluctantly. The chief lunged his body slightly toward Adam, but did not raise his hand. Adam had remained motionless. "I . . . I can't raise my hand!" exclaimed the chief, looking with disbelief as his unresponsive hand.

"No hand can harm me" stated Adam. "The heart would stop of any who would try to kill me. So would the hearts of any who would conspire with such a person in such an act. So, you can see, I'm quite safe. Your officers would be better used in traffic control."

"All the same" insisted the chief, "I'll have a few men stay in the vicinity."

"That would be fine" answered Adam.

The chief walked away, looking with curiosity at his hand which seemed to work fine now, but had failed him only seconds before. Pastor Kanger grinned as this was some new data that Adam hadn't shared with him before. The second news team saw its chance to take control of the interview.

Chapter 12 - The Departure

"Mr. Kanger, I'm Sue Bailey from TV32 News. Won't tomorrow bring suffering to many in the world? Is this God's way?"

"Miss Bailey, tomorrow will certainly bring discomfort to many. The physical discomfort should prompt mental discomfort as individuals ponder the reasons God is removing the use of their legs for a day. The events of tomorrow are necessary to open the eyes of many to God's way - to show them on a personal level they are betraying the trust of their fellow man."

Sue continued "I thought God was all about love and healing. Will God do some healing too?"

"Yes" responded Adam. "And Miss Bailey, YOU will be the first to make it happen - you will show the world how it is done."

"I think I need some more details" answered Sue, her brow wrinkled in puzzlement.

"The world first needs to get beyond Monday" answered Adam. "Tuesday morning, take me to someone you know to be sick or injured. We will proceed from there."

Adam walked away from the sudden focus of the media and found Pastor Kanger. The two walked through the city park as they had done back at the resort. Here, however, there was more open space . . . and considerably more people. After they had walked for a while and talked to hundreds of people, they returned to their car. They followed Jeff Gladding to his apartment to spend the night.

The apartment was indeed as small as advertised.

God's Gifts To Us All

~ Chapter 13 ~

A World Without Legs

Chapter 13 - A World Without Legs

When the sun rose on Monday, many people did not. A burning sensation in their right knee brought them out of their deep sleep. The pain would not allow them to rest. All ointments and other treatments were of no use. The leg was useless within an hour.

The reactions of people varied. Some took stock of their lives and pledged to make a new start. Others reacted in disbelief. They rationalized innocence of their past actions, since everyone else was doing the same thing. The 'everyone elses' of the world sat in similar paralysis - both of the body and of the mind. Thousands of people called hospitals and clinics. Nothing could be done.

Adam and Pastor Kanger were summoned from their sleep by the moaning sounds from Jeff Gladding. In the small apartment, it was clear that God was getting Jeff's attention. A couple of lights were switched on.

"My knee is on fire!" exclaimed young Jeff.

"Any idea why?" asked Adam who suddenly looked not to Jeff but to Pastor Kanger who had been sleeping on the sofa. The pastor was flexing his knee, and in realizing that he felt no symptoms, he let forth a sigh. Adam reached over and gave the pastor a couple of congratulatory pats on the back.

"TV reporting is very competitive" answered Jeff. "Sometimes I stretch some facts to make more of a story than was really there."

"Is that all?" asked Adam.

"Well . . . ouch" Jeff obviously didn't like the pain "I usually stretch some of the numbers on my income tax returns."

"Is THAT all?" asked Adam, glancing toward the pastor.

"I think I'll put on some coffee" remarked Arthur. "You two keep chatting."

"No, there's lots more!" confessed Jeff as he seemed to have a clear list of all the wrongs he had done.

For the next 45 minutes, Jeff told of faked sick days at work, taking coffee from the office pot without paying, and on it went. The list seemed so long that Arthur

Chapter 13 - A World Without Legs

and Adam looked toward each other several times and shook their heads slightly.

"An impressive list, Mr. Gladding" remarked Adam. "So what are you going to do about it?"

"It's clear to me it is all very wrong" said Jeff in remorse. "It was all too easy - THAT especially bothers me. I'm afraid I won't be strong enough to keep from doing it again."

"Have you heard my comments about prayer?" asked Adam.

Jeff thought for a few moments "Yes - I'm sure I saw that tape. Something about 'if you need some moments to regain your focus toward God's way' or something like that." Jeff's answer was phrased as half question and half statement.

"Pretty close!" said Adam. "When you feel a temptation in your path, just stop. Simply STOP! Take a moment or two to remember this day, your feelings at this moment. Think for a minute on what you understand to be God's way. You might be surprised how effective a few quiet seconds can be in the face of temptation. Add to that quiet reflection a positive attitude on your ability to walk God's path and you should never again feel like you do today."

Adam placed his hand on Jeff's shoulder. "Why don't you stay here today? I'll grab a quick shower then the padre and I need to go out and visit both the afflicted and the well."

"I'm not sure I have much choice!" responded Jeff. His right leg was now without feeling at all.

From the bathroom Adam answered "If you mean about today, you're probably right. If you are referring to the days to come, remember you will always have choices. Find the way to always make the right choices!" Adam closed the bathroom door.

As Adam and the pastor left the second story apartment, they looked out over what they could see of the city. Compared to the day before when people and

Chapter 13 - A World Without Legs

traffic were everywhere, this morning was quiet. There were a few cars visible and a few people here and there. "Maybe we should have turned on the TV!" commented Arthur.

"It would not have made any difference. Come, let's go!" said Adam as he descended the stairway. At the bottom was a familiar face. It was Lisa Walters.

"Good morning, Mr. Sampson" greeted Lisa.

"Good to see you again Miss Walters" responded Adam who looked around for other media teams. "You seem to be without any colleagues this morning."

Lisa replied apologetically "I'm embarrassed to say I couldn't even get an able-bodied cameraman from our studio this morning. This doesn't speak too well about my profession, does it?"

"No, I guess it doesn't" responded Adam. "On the other hand, your presence speaks volumes about YOUR personal character. I'm impressed by your inner strength . . . although I'm not surprised. Even Arthur here has remarked that your news pieces are fair and accurate. Well done!"

"Thanks" replied Lisa. "Have you watched any of the news this morning?"

"No, what's happening?" asked Arthur.

"Locally, the city has come to a standstill" reported Lisa. "No public transportation is running. Not many businesses are open. It's as if a giant snowstorm has blanketed the city, bringing things to a halt - except that it's a clear day in late summer" Lisa stopped herself as she felt like she was rambling on.

"How are the people taking things?" asked Adam.

"There's a very wide spectrum out there" answered Lisa. "Many of the churches opened their doors quite early this morning. Several are full of people who only have use of one leg."

"It will become more interesting at noon when they lose the use of their other leg" predicted Adam. "How about international reaction?"

Chapter 13 - A World Without Legs

"The last I heard from Japan, night was falling and people were regaining the use of their legs" reported Lisa. "Lots of confused people out there. They don't seem to know what to do."

"Why not go up to apartment 28?" suggested Adam. "Jeff Gladding up there can probably give you a few pointers you might want to share with your viewers."

Adam and pastor Kanger walked around the neighborhood for a while, then drove to different parts of the city. The lack of traffic made these cross town trips far easier then they would have been on any other Monday.

They returned to Jeff Gladding's apartment around dusk. Jeff was starting to get some feeling back in his legs.

"What a day!" exclaimed Jeff as he welcomed the two back in his apartment. "It's amazing what you can think about when you can't get anywhere! It was also amazing to turn on the TV every once in a while and see others around the world experiencing the same things!"

Jeff was standing with the help of the chairs around the table. He took a few baby steps with the chairs, then a few without. "It looks like such a nice evening, I think I'll go for a walk."

"Where will you go?" asked Adam.

"I haven't visited my neighbors for a long time and I never thanked the guy around the block who gave my car a jump start last winter. I just feel I want to be out with my neighbors. Then I want to drop by my parent's house for a quick visit. I know it's late, but I've been so busy lately, I haven't visited them for over a month! Make yourselves at home!" shouted Jeff as he bounded out the door on legs which had yet to gain their full strength.

Adam and the pastor looked at each other and smiled. Yes, God's plan was already showing results - and in Jeff, they were sure the results would be lasting.

God's Gifts To Us All

~ Chapter 14 ~

A Very Special Person

Chapter 14 - A Very Special Person

As Adam and Pastor Kanger awoke at Jeff Gladding's apartment, they could hear occasional muffled noises outside and noticed some flashes of light.

Jeff drew back a corner of the front window curtain and looked outside. "Oh, man! You should see all the people!" he exclaimed. Jeff blinked his eyes a few times in an effort to make sure he was awake and not just dreaming.

"You think God got the attention of some people, then?" asked Adam with a grin. Adam looked at the pastor with approval. Pastor Kanger shook his head slightly and returned Adam's smile - he was continually surprised at each new development with Adam.

"Come on, padre" directed Adam. "Let's get cleaned up and pack our things. It's time we moved on!"

"You're always welcome here!" declared Jeff who sat down. He took a breath as the excitement from looking out the window was being replaced by some more serious thoughts. "You know, I can't begin to thank you for the profound changes you have made in my life."

Adam replied, "What has Adam Sampson done? What has God done? Your pain and new insights yesterday were between you and God. I only told you it was going to happen and why."

"All the same, thanks" answered Jeff as he got up to shake Adam's hand.

As Adam and Pastor Kanger emerged from Jeff's apartment with their suitcases, the vision that greeted them was quite different compared to Monday's peace and quiet. Today, there was a sea of people in every direction. At the front was the media. Flashes from countless cameras went off time and again. Flood lights from the many TV crews blanketed the second story landing and the stairway toward the parking lot. Across the street, one camera operator was perched at the end of an elevated mechanical boom.

Adam had reached the top of the stairs, when there was a barrage of shouts from all the media at the same time. Each was trying to be the one to have their question answered. Adam looked at Pastor Kanger and shook his head in disgust. Ignoring the shouts from below, Adam paused at the head of the stairs

Chapter 14 - A Very Special Person

and the media became suddenly silent. They hadn't stopped trying to shout, they all just had no voice. They looked at each other and at their crews in disbelief. It was as if God paralyzed their voice boxes. In the background, some muffled applause was heard as the citizens approved with the actions taken.

"Members of the media, I will not be shouted at" announced Adam rather sternly. "When you have found your manners, then I will talk to you. For now, Pastor Kanger and I have places to go. Please excuse us."

Adam and the pastor worked their way past the still silent media and reached Arthur's car. With their baggage in the trunk, they climbed in. The police helped them back up carefully and leave the apartment complex. Once the car had reached the street, the media regained their voices. They combined packing their gear with blaming each other for 'getting in trouble'.

Pastor Kanger just drove rather aimlessly through the city until Adam started telling him where to turn. A growing media group was trying to follow, but the size of the group and the traffic lights limited the numbers that were able to keep up. Adam seemed to get more and more intent with each direction, like a hound on the path of its prey. Finally, with the car in the center of the 'bad part of town' Adam directed that Arthur pull over and stop.

The pastor caught himself about to ask Adam if he was sure about this. By now, the pastor understood that Adam's actions were with purpose and direction.

"Come on, padre" directed Adam. "There's someone I'd like you to meet."

As they got out of the car, media and police arrived in droves and began to follow Adam and the pastor as they entered a run down apartment building. They walked up to the third story. Adam slowly walked alone down the hallway ahead of the rest. He stopped at the door to apartment 308 and knocked.

A middle-aged woman answered the door. "Yes?" was the response by the surprised tenant.

"Mabel Jones?" asked Adam.

"Why yes!" answered the woman in surprise.

Chapter 14 - A Very Special Person

"I'm Adam Sampson and I'd like you to meet my friend Pastor Kanger" said Adam politely.

"You're him! You're the one, aren't you?" asked the woman, again in surprise. She then stuck her head out the door to see the hallway packed mostly by media. "Oh, my!" she exclaimed.

"I was wondering if we might come in and talk a while?" asked Adam.

"Why, yes!" responded Mabel. "Please come in." Mabel was trying to figure out just how many to let in, then just gave up and left the door open. "Please have a seat. These are my children, Donny and Laura."

Adam and the pastor each shook the hands of the children before taking a seat on the sofa. The small apartment wasn't fancy, but it was so clean and neat that Arthur was surprised. The small room was quickly filled with media, cameras and microphones.

"Adam, how is it you know Mrs. Jones?" asked the pastor in bewilderment.

"Know me?" asked Mabel. "I've never met any of you that I know of."

"God asked me to find you" reported Adam. "Please tell the group about your typical week."

Not really sure what she was getting in to, Mabel began. "Well, on Sundays I help down at the church getting things set up for the morning service. I join my sister who brings the kids and we all sit together for the service. The four of us usually come back here and visit for a while. After lunch, the kids and I go with some others from our church to visit the shut-in's around here. Some of us go to the senior citizens home for a while before returning to our homes. During the week, I've got a part time job at the restaurant a couple of blocks over. In the evening, it's pretty much the same thing - visiting people in the neighborhood - usually with others from our church." Mabel looked up at Adam to see if she was answering correctly.

Chapter 14 - A Very Special Person

"Mrs. Jones, do you have a $20 bill that I can borrow?" asked Adam. Pastor Kanger looked on with puzzlement since it was not like Adam to be asking for money.

"No sir" answered Mabel. "I'm a little short on cash right now - but I've got a 10 if you want it."

"What did you do with the last 20 you had?" asked Adam in a courtroom like manner.

"Last Friday I bought some out of date bread at the bakery down the street and gave it to some of the homeless over by the railroad" responded Mabel.

"Couldn't you have used that money on yourself?" asked Adam "Bought better food for you and the kids - or some new clothes?"

"We have what we need" answered Mabel, now really wondering what Adam was driving at. "I couldn't feel good about eating 'high' when I know so many have nothing at all."

"Mrs. Jones, you are truly a person of God!" proclaimed Adam. "You are doing everything you possibly can with all the gifts God has made available to you. You ignore your personal gains in favor of serving the less fortunate. You expect nothing in return. You implement your belief in God every day - in every way you know how. The world could learn a great deal from you."

Adam got up from the sofa and shook Mabel's hand. "We must be going" said Adam. "Let me know if there is anything I can do to help you."

"From what I have been able to see, you know exactly what to do to help everyone" said Mabel. "Don't give up!"

"I promise you I won't" answered Adam who squeezed out the door.

The first media asked Adam a question, but Adam didn't answer. Instead he asked what the reporter had done that day to make the world a better place. The reporter said he couldn't think of anything. Adam responded "Let's change

**God's
Gifts
To
Us All**

~ Chapter 15 ~

How To Heal

Chapter 15 - How To Heal

Adam and the pastor followed Sue Bailey's car to a hospital parking lot on the east side of town. They parked their cars and were joined by some of the people who had followed them through the streets of the city. Waiting in the parking lot was a couple of mobile unit trucks from Sue's TV station.

"What have you got here?" asked Adam as he got out of the car next to Sue's open door.

"A burn victim, Melissa Meyers" answered Sue. "There was an apartment fire two nights ago we covered on the late night news and I remembered about a 12-year-old girl who had been seriously burned. They have her here in the special burn unit."

"Sounds like a good candidate!" remarked Adam. "Let's go!"

One of Sue's crew was following them pretty close. "Do you mind the crew being this close?" asked Sue.

"No, not today" answered Adam. "It's very important that what happens here today is recorded accurately."

Inside the lobby they were met by Dr. O'Connor. After introductions the doctor warned "I need to know what you have planned. I can't take any chances of infection."

"I need to have Miss Bailey, myself, and at least one camera crew at the side of Melissa" said Adam. "If none of the burn is exposed, I would like to uncover some of it so we can see if we are making progress. Miss Bailey will need to touch the girl somewhere on her body but it doesn't have to be the burn area. The whole process shouldn't take more than 20 minutes or so."

The doctor turned to speak with some of the others of the medical staff who had gathered. After a few moments and some gesturing, the doctor answered "We normally would not allow this sort of thing, but because of what we have seen and heard about Mr. Sampson, we will make an exception. Instead of bringing your equipment into the burn room, we will empty an adjoining room where you can set up. We will wheel Melissa in when you're ready."

Chapter 15 - How To Heal

It took several minutes for the room to be emptied and the crew to get set up. Adam, the doctor and Sue walked through where the girl's bed would be parked, and how the cameras would be arranged to get the scene. Adam seemed to be very intent on making sure the media got quality footage of what was about to happen. Finally they were ready.

Melissa and her bed were wheeled into the designated parking spot. "Doctor, I'd like you to expose some of the burned tissue" directed Adam. "If we do something you object to, just say the word and we will stop."

The doctor cut away and unwrapped some of the gauze on the girl's right hand. There was noticeable reddening and then some blisters as more of the covering was removed.

"How's this?" asked the doctor.

"Fine" replied Adam. "Miss Bailey, please hold Melissa's left hand."

Sue inched toward the bed and held the girl's unaffected left hand. The girl was in a state of semi-consciousness, mostly due to the medications. "Now what?"

"You will need to clear your mind of all distractions and then you will tell Melissa that you are accepting responsibility for her burns" stated Adam.

"What exactly should I say?" asked Sue.

"God will give you the words" Adam answered. Adam looked around to make sure the cameras, microphones, and lights were correctly positioned. "Would everyone be quiet please? Miss Bailey needs to concentrate."

Sue closed her eyes.

"That's good" whispered Adam. "Empty your mind and open your heart to God's helping hand."

Sue continued with her eyes closed in the hushed room. She seemed to sway back and forth slightly, then opened her eyes slowly. "I believe in God and the vast powers of God." There was a pause of several seconds, then Sue continued softly "I believe I can make a difference in this world with my life. Melissa, your

Chapter 15 - How To Heal

burns are being cured as God and I work together on your behalf." Another pause. "Today I am devoting my life to God's work for the sake of your health. If I stray from God's path, your burns will return as they are today. May I find the strength to stay true to God's way."

Adam then spoke quietly "The healing should only take a few moments. Miss Bailey you may start to feel a bit strange."

In a matter of seconds, the blisters disappeared and the red vanished as if a covering of frost was quickly evaporating. "Dear God!" remarked the doctor.

"Quite correct" said Adam. "You should be able to remove all the bandages now."

Sue Bailey took several steps backwards and stood by Adam.

The doctor and some nurses stepped in and began to cut and unwrap. They continuously remarked to each other that this area or that was one that was charred badly and yet the skin looked good as new. Doctor O'Connor stooped over and looked very close at Melissa's skin. "I don't believe it!" exclaimed the doctor. "I've never seen anything like this before!"

"It's just energy conversion" explained Adam.

"What?!" responded the doctor in bewilderment.

"Remember back to your college days. Weren't mass and energy really the same thing?" asked Adam. "How much energy would you have if you converted all of the mass of the human body into energy?"

"I don't know for sure, but as I remember it, a tiny amount of mass is equivalent to tremendous amounts of energy" answered the doctor, looking upwards in an effort to better remember his college physics.

"Right" said Adam. "With God's help, a tiny bit of matter from Sue Bailey was converted into the energy needed to heal Melissa's burns. Do you feel all right Miss Bailey?"

"Yes, fine" remarked Sue. "Maybe a little light headed, that's all."

Chapter 15 - How To Heal

"Good" replied Adam. "Now comes the hard part. If you stray from God's way, Melissa's burns will return as quickly as they disappeared. You will need to stay strong, but it's a wonderful thing you have done!"

"Praise God!" came from the side of the room as Melissa's parents rushed to her side to help remove her bandages.

"Was this recorded?" asked Adam of the camera crew.

"Yes" said one of the technicians. "We are sending out live transmissions on the network at this moment."

Adam turned to face the cameras "On Monday the world felt one of the hands of God as they lost the use of their legs because they were betraying the trust of their fellow man. When the sun comes up this Thursday, the world will feel the loving hand of God. Worldwide, everyone will have the ability to heal anyone of any sickness, disease, or affliction, just like you saw here. Remember to make the healing last, you must stay true to God. If you slip, you must go to the person you wronged, tell them what you did that was wrong, and ask their forgiveness. After the sun goes down on Thursday, you can only slip twice. After that, the person will be just as they were before you healed them and you will not be able to alter their situation."

"Go now!" directed Adam. "Get this word to the far corners of the earth. It's a great opportunity you should not pass up!"

Adam and the pastor talked to the medical staff and many of the patients. Dr. O'Connor asked Adam and the pastor to spend the night at his house. They accepted.

**God's
Gifts
To
Us All**

~ Chapter 16 ~

What About The Wealthy?

Chapter 16 - What About The Wealthy?

Dr. O'Connor's home was very large, especially when compared to Jeff Gladding's apartment. The house was nestled in a wooded lot in the suburbs. All of the homes in the area were similar in nature. The people who lived here definitely had to have considerable wealth to afford such splendor.

Dr. O'Connor's wife Margaret met Adam and the pastor when they pulled in the drive, following the doctor's car.

"Welcome to our home!" exclaimed Margaret, bursting in delight to the point that she wasn't really sure what to do with all her energy. "When my husband called and said you would be staying with us tonight, I couldn't believe it! I wish I had more time to prepare our guest rooms for you and clean the house a little better!"

"Mrs. O'Connor, we have come to visit with you, not these structures" responded Adam. "Everything will be fine - please relax."

Adam and the pastor were unloading their bags from the trunk of the car when a police car drove up. A detective got out and asked "You want the media kept out or let in on your property?"

The doctor looked at Adam and said "I'd prefer they stay out, but I will go along with Mr. Sampson's wishes."

"Tonight, please keep them off the property" replied Adam. "We need some quiet, quality time to discuss many things."

"You got it!" replied the detective who reached for his radio as he got in the car and backed out of the drive. Everyone else walked into the doctor's house.

"If you don't mind, I've invited a couple of the neighbors and a couple friends over for dinner" stated Mrs. O'Connor to both Adam and her husband, partly as a question.

"Margaret!" sighed the doctor. "I thought we could have a quiet evening . . . alone!"

Chapter 16 - What About The Wealthy?

"It's fine with me" answered Adam. "I'd like the opportunity to meet your friends and neighbors."

Adam and the pastor placed their things in the rooms which had been readied for them. Before long, they were at the dinner table with the friends and neighbors the doctor's wife had invited.

As they were served the first course, everyone looked around nervously, wondering if someone should say a prayer. Finally the doctor's wife spoke "Mr. Sampson, would you like to say grace?"

"Please, proceed with the meal like you always do. If you usually say a prayer, go ahead and do so. If you usually don't, go ahead with the meal. You won't offend me in either case" responded Adam.

Margaret offered a rather makeshift prayer, trying to convince Adam and her guests that she did that all the time. Adam grinned toward the pastor as the forced prayer was easily recognized as something the O'Connors usually didn't do.

Most of the dinner was spent with Adam asking the friends and neighbors about their families, professions, and their favorite vacation spots.

Interspersed with this light conversation, Adam remarked as each course was served about the plants and animals which had to die to provide the meal. He then posed rhetorical questions to the group if they were doing things with their lives that could justify the deaths they had paid for - were they worthy of the nourishment they were taking.

Adam also offered as one of God's great gifts the digestive system - able to convert energy from food into energy we can control. Adam remarked that in the days to come, people would experience other forms of energy conversion. Everyone exchanged puzzled facial expressions, but nobody was brave enough to ask Adam what he was talking about. As well educated individuals, they didn't want to ask any 'dumb' questions. Unfortunately, they let an educational opportunity slip by.

After dinner they got up and moved to the living room.

Chapter 16 - What About The Wealthy?

Doctor O'Connor remarked to Adam that he wondered how God 'felt' about wealthy people.

"The answer can be found in two questions" said Adam. "How did you acquire your wealth? What are you doing with your wealth?"

"In any society, there will always be some people with more wealth, some with less" continued Adam. "If you worked harder or smarter than your fellow man, you probably earned your wealth in a way which was pleasing to God. If you earned your wealth by cheating your fellow man, taking advantage of his misfortunes, or not performing up to the trust others have placed in you, you probably experienced some leg problems last Monday as God provided you some direct feedback on those methods of acquiring wealth."

"Once you have some wealth, what should you do with it?" asked Adam. "While spending some on yourself is understandable, too many wealthy people treat themselves too well. They compete with their fellow wealthy friends in vain attempts to out spend each other on status symbols. They have lost perspective as to what the potential their wealth has to make a positive difference in the world."

"Many of us contribute to several charities and churches" retorted Doctor O'Connor. "Doesn't that count for something?"

"Maybe" answered Adam. "Most contributions are done to purchase a clear conscience. Most of you contribute the least amount you think you can get away with. Few of you hold your charity accountable for the money you contribute - because you don't really care. Many of you do it just for a tax advantage."

"Take your 'charity money' and spend it directly yourself in a good cause" directed Adam. "Watch it do some good personally. Go back to the places you made better from time to time and make sure they are still the way they should be. Find some deserving people who need some financial help to find their dreams. Find some undeserving people and find a way to turn their lives around. Don't do these things for the tax advantage or to outperform each other. Do it because it's the right thing to do. Do it with the belief that you will be the only one to know what you did. You will feel God's grace fill your heart and soul when you begin to use your wealth in this way."

Chapter 16 - What About The Wealthy?

Adam continued "Think about the time and money each of you spent on your lawns last year. Chances are your involvement with your lawn was more extensive than your involvement with your community. Think about it. . . . Are your priorities where they should be? Instead of nurturing the perfect lawn, you could be nurturing the perfect community."

Adam then asked the group "How many poor people do you know as friends? How many have you helped financially? What about middle class people? How many have you had over for dinner? Have you helped any put a child through school?" Adam paused for several seconds. "There are multitudes out there who would benefit from your wealth and wisdom. Go out and find them. Be their sponsor. Help them however you can. But be sure to hold them accountable to make the best of the help you share with them."

"Mr. Sampson, there's a phone call for you" said Margaret O'Connor. "A Mabel Jones. You can take it in the next room."

Adam left for a few minutes while the rest talked about what Adam has just related to them. When Adam returned, most hung their heads, ashamed about the way they had acquired their wealth or what they were doing with it - or both!

"That was Mabel Jones" said Adam. "The pastor and I met her on Tuesday. As an example of what we just discussed, this woman used her last $20 bill to buy bread she gave to the homeless on the poor side of town. Convert the $20 bill in her life to the resources you have control over, and you can begin to grasp the magnitude your efforts need to be. How many homeless could YOU feed? What other things could you do with your money to make people, places, and things better than they were when you found them? As you drive to and from the city, find the things that need fixing, then find the time and money to make it happen."

Adam turned to Pastor Kanger. "Pastor, we need to return to Mabel Jones' neighborhood tomorrow. She has taken us up on our offer to help her. Any of you care to come along?"

About half of the group said they would. The rest said they had schedules that would not allow them to participate.

Chapter 16 - What About The Wealthy?

Adam reported that they would be leaving at 9am the next morning. Adam also reported that they would be going after a drug dealing bully who was causing Mabel Jones' neighborhood to live in fear. Most who said they would go along exchanged worried looks at each other.

Margaret O'Connor announced she would have a brunch ready at 8am for any who were interested.

God's
Gifts
To
Us All

~ Chapter 17 ~

A Very Lost Sheep

Chapter 17 - A Very Lost Sheep

As morning broke the O'Connor residence was busy. Adam and the pastor were collecting their things and some of the friends arrived to sample Margaret's brunch. The police continued to keep the masses at a distance.

With everyone ready, they got in their cars and started off. The crowd around the estate quickly faded away and many went to their cars in an attempt to follow Adam. As usual, several media groups were ready when Adam's group left and kept up a close pursuit.

The group found their way to the projects where Mabel lived and parked their cars. Adam took the lead and walked toward a tall apartment building across the street. As Adam neared the front of the building, a man who was leaning against a parked car approached.

"Hey! What you want, man?" demanded the character, attempting to block Adam's way.

"I have come for Jamahl Washington" responded Adam.

"Maybe Jamahl don't want to see you!" answered the man sarcastically. Some of the media had arrived, but the police contingent was not to be seen yet.

"I have come to free Jamahl from his wicked ways and to set the neighborhood free" retorted Adam with defiance. Adam then side stepped the man and headed for the front door of the complex.

In response to Adam's side step the character pivoted the opposite way and pulled a gun from his jacket. The character had not quite extended his shooting arm when he suddenly dropped the gun in a patch of grass next to the sidewalk. His knees gave out on him and he fell on his back in the middle of the sidewalk. On his face was a look of terror. His hands clutched his chest. There was a gasp of horror from the group.

Adam turned to see him. "In your attempt to take my life, you have taken your own instead."

Adam then looked toward the group which was following him "Look upon God's power over man! The doctors will find his heart has exploded. Come, let's bring

Chapter 17 - A Very Lost Sheep

the light of God to his friends in this place!" Adam turned and walked up the front steps and entered the building. The others paused for a few moments, then carefully stepped around the lifeless body and followed Adam inside.

One of the tenants was in the front lobby, checking a mail box. Adam addressed her, "Excuse me, could you tell me where we might find Jamahl Washington?"

The middle-aged woman looked at Adam and then the others who were trickling in the front door. "Go to 402 - but be careful!" she warned.

Adam quickly found the stairs and began the ascent to the fourth floor. "Don't you just love how a couple flights of stairs can help you fill the depths of your lungs with oxygen?" Adam remarked to the pastor and the others. "Too many people take the act of breathing for granted - but it's one of God's great designs - gives our blood the oxygen it needs while getting rid of our waste gasses."

At last they were on the fourth floor. Adam stood in front of the door marked '402' and knocked. After a period of silence, Adam knocked again. Finally a deep voice responded behind the closed door "Yeah! Who's there?"

Adam answered "Some of God's children. We have come for Jamahl Washington."

The voice answered back "Uhm . . . Jamahl's not here today - sorry. Maybe you could come back sometime."

Adam kept the pressure up "Mr. Washington, your sentry down below died minutes ago at the hand of God when he tried to pull a gun on me. I think you had better open your door so we can talk."

Some footsteps could be heard inside the apartment as it sounded like someone was going to a window to look out. A muffled woman's voice could be heard shouting across the apartment "It's Billy! He's gone!"

After some more commotion inside the apartment, the door cracked open. "What you want with me?" asked a deep voice.

"May we come in?" asked Adam.

Chapter 17 - A Very Lost Sheep

"Suppose so" answered Jamahl who opened the door all the way.

Jamahl Washington was a giant of a man. He towered over Adam and the others. He was wearing a T-shirt which showed his muscular build. His head was rather block shaped and his eyes showed a life of hard times - and yet a stubborn arrogance as well.

"Mr. Washington, I'm Adam Sampson and this is Pastor Kanger" started Adam.

"How you know me?" asked Jamahl.

"A friend told me you make life difficult in this part of town - you beat up kids and take their money, you rob anyone who walks the streets, and you circulate drugs to kids as well as adults" said Adam.

"You can't prove none of that" said Jamahl, suddenly aware of a TV camera which had followed Adam into the apartment.

"I'm not here to prove the past" said Adam. "I have come to help you make a different future for yourself and for your community."

"Why should I?" asked Jamahl. "I like my girls, my boys, and I even like my habits. It ain't such a bad life."

"Tell you what" offered Adam. "I'll arm wrestle you for it. You win, we will leave and not say a word. I win, and you will let the pastor and I spend the night here."

"That's all?" asked Jamahl. "No tricks?"

"No tricks, honest" replied Adam.

"Don't do it Jam!" came a woman's voice from an adjoining bedroom. "He'll trick you for sure!"

"Shut up, woman!" commanded Jamahl. "This here 150 pound chump is about to get his butt whipped!"

Adam and Jamahl walked over to a table in the room and sat facing each other.

Chapter 17 - A Very Lost Sheep

"You understand I have God on my side" cautioned Adam. "I'd understand if you wanted to back down."

"No need" retorted the giant. "I got over 300 pounds on my side!"

As the two joined hands to begin the contest, Adam's smaller hand just seemed to disappear into Jamahl's.

Adam sat calmly, looking into Jamahl's dark eyes. "Start whenever you're ready" said Adam. The TV crew was positioned to record the event.

With a grunt and a lunge, Jamahl threw his weight behind his grip. His back muscles rippled under his shirt. However, shooting from his shoulder to his fingertips was an unexplained burst of nervous impulses which left the giant's arm limp as a rag. A look of surprise took over his face as his arm felt like the crazy bone had been smashed.

"You can't possibly win, Mr. Washington" said Adam. "You can always beat me alone, but you can never beat me when God is by my side!" Adam gently pushed Jamahl's hand to the table. Adam grinned at Pastor Kanger and remarked "Padre, it looks like we'll be spending the night with Mr. Washington!"

Jamahl stood up from the table, rubbing his arm. "I don't have no feelings in my arm. How'd you do that?"

"Here, I can make it feel better" said Adam, reaching out both his hands "Hold my hands."

The two stood facing each other. Adam closed his eyes for a few moments and a hush fell over the apartment.

"Jamahl, tomorrow will be a day of great healing all over the world. People everywhere will join forces with God to heal the sick, give sight to the blind, and mend the broken bones. I need your help to reach those who may be in need. Therefore, today it is by my faith in God that we begin the healing process in you. The pain in your arm is gone. Your habits are gone. Your cravings for power, domination and wealth are gone as well. Your heart and mind are pure. You are

Chapter 17 - A Very Lost Sheep

now ready for God's great work! May you always find the inner strength to stay true to God."

Adam then released Jamahl's hands. At first Jamahl's arms dropped by his side. He lifted his right hand and looked at it carefully. He flexed it a few times. Next, he flexed both hands. Jamahl shifted his view from his hands over toward Adam. "I feel great! I've never felt like this before!"

"That's what it feels like when God has touched your soul! Do you feel you need any guns or drugs?" asked Adam, testing this new convert.

"No . . . , not at all" said Jamahl slowly, acting very surprised that he was able to make that statement. "Let me give you all that I have."

Jamahl disappeared into one of the bedrooms and returned. Four pistols, a sawed off shotgun and an assault rifle were placed on the table along with several boxes of ammo. Jamahl disappeared again and returned with several bags. Each had a different variety of drug, except one bag which held a large sum of money.

"I don't feel like I need any of this anymore!" said Jamahl. Upon hearing Jamahl's words, his disgusted girlfriend stormed out of the apartment without a word.

"Padre, would you carefully transport these things to our police escorts down on the street?" asked Adam. "Jamahl and I will need the bag of money to visit a friend of ours."

Adam left the apartment with Jamahl and the bag of money. They walked the couple blocks over to Mabel Jones' apartment. When she opened the door, Jamahl said he wanted her to have the money to buy bread for the poor. Tears instantly consumed the woman's eyes as she looked over at Adam.

She knew God had won a great victory that day.

**God's
Gifts
To
Us All**

~ Chapter 18 ~

A Day Of Healing

Chapter 18 - A Day Of Healing

The day of healing was one of the most glorious days the world had ever known. People everywhere reached out to their fellow man, proclaimed their faith in God, and took personal responsibility for the healing of all sorts of ailments and afflictions.

The joy in the healers was as great as the joy in those being healed. Almost everyone felt an awaking of their spirit they had never felt before. Tears of happiness flooded the world as the deaf found their hearing, the blind their sight. Diseases of all descriptions mysteriously vanished. Even those healers who lost their way with God during the day and were forced to confess what they had done, felt such a burst of renewal that they began to think seriously about their lifestyle and the true ways of God.

In the city Adam, Jamahl, and Pastor Kanger toured the inner city early in the morning. They visited all the haunts that Jamahl knew and helped thousands begin a fresh, healthy life with God. They also kept the local police units busy with the drugs and guns they collected. Later the trio went to several dozen stops around the city. They mostly witnessed others in the act of healing. In some cases, they joined hands with the homeless or some forgotten people in the hospitals of the area. All glowed with the fire of God's presence and reveled in their new found feelings of wellness.

At the end of the day the three returned to Jamahl's apartment for some well-deserved rest.

The hearts, the minds, the souls of the world were filled with God's grace.

God's Gifts To Us All

~ Chapter 19 ~

The Planning Session

Chapter 19 - The Planning Session

Adam, Jamahl and Pastor Kanger drove to the TV studio on the north edge of the city for a meeting that Lisa Walters had set up. Pastor Kanger was a little surprised that Adam had agreed to meet with a festival promoter. He was even more surprised when Adam asked Lisa to have an author present as well.

Soon the trio was inside one of the conference rooms and Lisa introduced them to a group of promoters. The leader of the group began "My company is interested in arranging an outdoor festival of sorts on your behalf - a sort of *A Day With Adam Sampson*. We would have some musical acts, you could talk from time to time - we would have a Woodstock type event. What do you think?"

Adam answered "I like the concept, but I must insist on a number of changes and stipulations. First, it needs to be *A Day With God*. The focus needs to be on God, not on me. Next, everything must be free to the more than one million attendees. No admission, no charge for food or drink - everything is free. No advertising, no hype - for it to be *A Day With God*, it needs to be simple, yet powerful."

The promoter replied "I'm not sure we can do that. We would be able to market the film of the event, the sound track, or the TV feeds, right?"

Adam responded instantly "Absolutely not! Everything is free - everything is donated, from the materials, talent, the equipment, everything! All recordings of any kind will be free for anyone. No royalties, revenues or profits are to come from *A Day With God*!" Adam fixed a piercing stare at the spokesman for the group.

"I don't really see why we should invest in such a venture?" said the leader as he looked at his companions.

Adam countered "Will you pass up the opportunity to host and record the most talked about event in recent history?"

The leader responded with a stammer "We . . . ah we will have to get back to you about something like this."

Chapter 19 - The Planning Session

"Noon tomorrow" replied Adam. "Unless I hear a 'Yes' from you by then, I will go to your competition and they will go down in history books as the hosts for the event."

"Where's the author?" queried Adam of Lisa.

"Over here" responded Lisa. "Adam Sampson, I'd like you to meet Michael Brown."

"Mr. Brown, pleased to meet you" greeted Adam as he quickly shifted gears from his stern behavior with the promoters.

"Mr. Brown, I'd like you to chronicle the events about God's messages I have been delivering and the events to come. Pastor Kanger has been keeping a journal which should be a great help to you."

The writer looked up from the notes he was taking and accepted the offer "I would be glad to. Judging from your interaction with the promoters, I'll bet there are some conditions or stipulations."

"You're right!" chuckled Adam as he glanced toward Pastor Kanger.

"First of all" began Adam "the book you write needs to be about God and not about me. You need to write it in a simple, easy to read style so that people of all ages and social classes can read it and understand. The simplicity will also make it easy to translate into the other languages of the world. Have it published by the best in the business - create a book which can be read again and again - which can be passed from generation to generation. Learn from the ancient manuscripts about God. Tell a timeless story which will continue to be valid as times and people change. Tell a story which will always bring people back to God and once back to God, keep their faith alive and fresh."

The author was busy taking notes and holding a small tape recorder as a back up. "Sounds like a challenging opportunity! Anything else?"

"Yes" replied Adam rather sternly. "With this book" Adam turned his head to the group of promoters who were listening nearby "and with any type of enterprise, guard yourself from becoming rich from your efforts. Large sums of money may

Chapter 19 - The Planning Session

come your way - a modest income is fine, but if you don't share the wealth gained from promoting God - use the money to make the world a better place - you and your family will suffer great pain. History will record you as a profiteer and people will doubt the truth of the story you tell - believing it all a ploy to increase sales. Remember this, and make good decisions - or don't be surprised by the consequences."

"I'll try to remember that" replied the author, jotting another note. "When do we begin?"

"At once" replied Adam. "You and pastor Kanger need to get together and go over his journal. You should also be prepared to do some traveling with us to accurately record new developments."

The author walked off to the side with Pastor Kanger and the two started talking quietly but at a rapid pace. The pastor was trying to tell an overview of his association with Adam Sampson and the author was trying to jot notes just as fast as he could.

Adam turned to look at the promoters, who suddenly felt a sharp contrast between the author's acceptance of Adam's proposal and their earlier rejection. The promoters looked toward the floor to avoid eye contact with Adam. They mumbled to each other as they turned and left the conference room.

**God's
Gifts
To
Us All**

~ Chapter 20 ~

Travels Across The Country

Chapter 20 - Travels Across The Country

Early the next morning, Adam was contacted by the promoters who had reluctantly agreed to put on *A Day With God*. Adam complimented them on their wisdom and told them he was planning on making a tour of the country while the promoters were making all the arrangements. Adam accepted a cellular phone from the leader of the promotion group to keep informed of developments in the program and to make a host of logistical decisions.

After completing their business in the city, Adam, Pastor Kanger, Jamahl, and the author departed for a tour of the country. A local car dealer had donated a custom van to Adam after seeing how poorly Jamahl fit into the pastor's car. The van allowed the foursome to travel in comfort and actively discuss what they had done or were going to do. Each of the group took a turn driving at some time during their travels.

Following Adam's group was a variable sized array of media trucks and private citizen vehicles. In some states and counties they were joined by large police escorts. At other times, the group seemed to be without any police escort.

The first few days resulted in stops at several farms along the way. Adam seemed to enjoy the open country air. While touring one large dairy barn Adam remarked "Farmers are among the closest to God and God's works. Everywhere you look, you see processes which perform energy conversions according to God's great designs. Look at the sun, the soil, the crops, the animals - each evidence of God's great engineering!"

The group next visited several urban areas in the path of their travels. In the cities, Jamahl was regarded as some sort of folk hero. He wasn't a polished speaker, yet his slow soft delivery carried with it such great force he was able to get large groups of people to take action. He was especially loved by the inner city youth. On several occasions, Jamahl led cleanup-fixup sweeps in an area of urban decay. The pastor and Adam watched from the sidelines as this giant, who was once a cancer on society - took a slum and made it better - and also offered words of encouragement to the residents about how to fight to keep it from slipping into decay. He had been there himself. He knew.

At one point in their travels, Adam asked the author where he would like to visit. "A National Park" was the answer and after checking their supply of road maps, they found themselves at an extensive wildlife preserve. Since they had good

Chapter 20 - Travels Across The Country

weather, they went for a hike on one of the trails. They didn't see much wildlife as the foursome was joined by the noise of several mobile TV crews and about a hundred assorted others. After three or four miles they rested by a stream. Adam and several others removed their shoes and socks to soak their feet in the cool waters.

"Why do we have so few areas like this?" asked Adam rather rhetorically. "In some shape or form, it usually gets back to greed. Too many people allow the acquisition of wealth to guide their decision making processes. In the few cases where the focus is not 'what's in it for me?' - and people have taken the approach 'what can we do for others - today and in the future?' - some very special places - like this - have been set aside. It's never too late to begin creating other parks like this."

Pastor Kanger saw an opportunity for a question that had puzzled him for some time. "Adam, as I see your feet in the water, I'm curious about your thoughts about baptism."

"In many ways, baptism is really no different than any other religious ritual. How it's performed, its meaning and value depend largely on the individual and the circumstances. For me, it marked a new beginning - a sudden and personal relationship with God. As you may recall, you selected some special words for my ritual. They were right for me and my situation."

Adam continued "Baptism is certainly not any requirement. People find God in many different ways. Some find God by themselves. Others find God with a helping hand from someone else. Often, this helping hand is direct like I experienced with you. Many, however, get help in finding God from others long ago through their writings in ancient manuscripts."

Adam concluded "The path you take to find God is really not important. The important thing is that somehow you find God. Many children grow up being told that they believe in God, but never find God for themselves - on their own terms - as a significant part of their lives - and God never becomes an important part of their value system. For some, like me, it takes a bolt of lightning to discover God. For many, God is discovered by seeing something familiar - often something simple - in a new way. Once God's grand design is seen in one thing, it is soon seen in everything. I guarantee you will always remember that first day

Chapter 20 - Travels Across The Country

you found God, established a personal relationship, and started to believe - and consequently started to better understand life."

Adam concluded "After you have found God, the next thing is to make use of the gifts God has made available to you to make the world a better place."

Jamahl asked the next question. "Are we really the center of God's attention?"

"Jamahl," began Adam "man has long held a belief that he has been the center of everything. In ancient times, they believed that earth was the center of the solar system, the solar system the center of the galaxy, and our galaxy the center of the universe. We now know our physical place in the cosmos is not in the center. It doesn't mean we don't exist. It doesn't mean we are any more important that the rest of the stars and planets - only that we are part of a bigger whole. Our relationship with God is much the same. God has no favorites or priorities as humans do. We are part of the bigger whole to God - not unimportant - but not the only thing either."

One of the citizens asked "There's quite a stir in the religious communities about your comments that parts of the ancient holy books may not really represent God's word - that they contain false statements - lies if you will. Is it your intention to create this turmoil?"

Adam thought for a moment and responded "Lies are lies - truth is truth. A lie shouted from the rooftops, believed by an entire civilization, recorded in beautiful manuscripts, and passed down through hundreds of generations . . . is still a lie." Adam then spoke quietly "The whispered truth by one person which nobody records will always be the truth."

Another citizen asked "Mr. Sampson, how would we go about ending the conflicts around the world?"

Again Adam took a few moments to ponder the issue and collect his thoughts "While there is no perfect answer to all situations, I'll offer two suggestions. The first is to understand similarities and differences. Opposing factions should take some time to formally list all the values they share, as well as the values they disagree over. It's often surprising to see how similar two groups are who think they have nothing in common. It's also disappointing to think about the conflicts

Chapter 20 - Travels Across The Country

through the ages which happened where nobody took the time to clearly understand the issues - and often fought over nothing."

"The second suggestion is to keep fighting until victory. You must understand that 'victory' is a solution to conflict without the need to resort to physical force. As a result, 'fighting' is the process of achieving the 'victory'. You will need to engage the wisest, most talented and patient from all sides to clearly define the issues and find innovative ways to resolve the conflict. Such idea fighting can be every bit as difficult as physical fighting. To really be effective, participants need to fight as hard for their opponent's ideas as they do for their own. A complete victory is achieved when everybody wins."

The group gathered their things and was soon back on the highway.

From time to time on their journey, Adam talked on the cellular phone to the promoters. Adam's group often met with the promoters along their way, viewed audition tapes of the musical acts, listened to tapes of selected speakers, read manuscripts of material to be presented, and went over details of the gathering. Adam's remarks about the proposed event material became well known to everyone since they were always the same. He required that the focus to be on the song that was being sung or material being read - and not the performance. The songs and material could not promote any religion. They were to attest to the profound influence God has in our lives, the need for us to care for our natural resources, and the need for us to work together to make the world a better place. Adam required the performers dress in a simple manner and have a delivery that encouraged the audience to think about the words or share in the singing. Any efforts to bring the focus on the performer would not be acceptable.

Finally, all the details had been worked out and their journey had come to an end. It was time for *A Day With God*.

**God's
Gifts
To
Us All**

~ Chapter 21 ~

Preparations

Chapter 21 - Preparations

The preparations for *A Day With God* were staggering. In addition to building the stages and the media towers, there were countless other details to attend to. The public transportation, seating, refreshments, and restrooms all had to be addressed and result in no charges to the attendees. In conjunction with these aspects of the event, 800,000 pairs of free tickets had to be given away in a raffle which ensured the even and impartial distribution that Adam had insisted upon.

The promoters obtained access to a gentle canyon area where a stage complex was built at the lower end. The gradual slope provided an unobstructed view of the stage area for anyone seated. The canyon width was also ideal for the placement of the stage. The canyon walls were rounded with age and had numerous gaps which would serve as arteries to get people in and out. The sparse covering of prairie grass required little preparation for the event. An interstate highway exit was less than a mile from the site. Things seemed perfect.

The central stage complex was built with three joined stages. This allowed one group or presenter to be performing while the next set up on a different stage.

The setting and the size of the crowd required an extensive sound system as well as a system of large video screens to allow even the most remote seats to have a good view of what was happening on stage.

Everything was ready.

**God's
Gifts
To
Us All**

~ Chapter 22 ~

A Day With God - Performances

Chapter 22 - *A Day With God* - Performances

The weather was perfect. All of the logistical planning had paid off. The immense gathering covered the canyon to make it look like it had been painted with a grand mosaic. The media helicopters and planes had completed their aerial shots and had departed according to Adam's instructions. Everyone took their seats and the master of ceremonies got things started.

"Welcome everyone to this *Day With God*. Our first musical act is ready to begin. Feel free to join in the singing. Each of you should have your free event book which contains all the lyrics and text for today's material. We hope you enjoy the day and remember to refrain from applause - we are here to learn and understand, not to be entertained."

With those few remarks, the first group began their song. They were followed by the reading of a poem. The third presenter read a tribal story about the relationship of the earth, the animals, and man. And so the day went. It was a most diverse collection of legends, poetry and songs - from all the corners of the globe - some contemporary, some ancient - and yet it somehow all seemed to be related.

Adam's remarks over the weeks were having an effect. People were beginning to see how close together the world's beliefs and values really were. They saw present day relevance in stories from long ago. When they experienced a difference with others, they were taking time to understand if it was a common concept but expressed with a different name or described using different terminology. People also began to readily see the aspects of their inherited beliefs and values which encouraged aggressive behavior toward others who were not exactly the same. For the first time in their lives, many of the attendees were able to look at another culture with respect and understanding.

It was late afternoon when they reached the point in the program where Adam was scheduled to speak. The master of ceremonies announced there would be another 30 minute break. A muffled din came from the large crowd as people stood up, walked around, and talked with one another.

As Adam prepared to take the stage, he came over to Jamahl, Pastor Kanger, the author, and Lisa Walters who stood in a group off to one side. "Your friendship has meant everything to me. When I am gone, find strength in each other and in God. I love each of you very much."

Chapter 22 - *A Day With God* - Performances

As Adam walked toward the stage, the group exchanged puzzled looks at each other. Finally Pastor Kanger shouted "What do you mean 'when you're gone'?"

Adam paused at the edge of the stage and removed his shoes and socks but did not respond to the pastor's question. Adam only smiled.

It was time.

**God's
Gifts
To
Us All**

~ Chapter 23 ~

Adam Speaks

Chapter 23 - Adam Speaks

A hush fell upon the sea of people as Adam walked to the microphones.

"Children of God" began Adam, "welcome to this day of God! I'd like to thank all of the fine musicians, readers and performers who shared their talents with you today. I'd also like to thank the organizers and sponsors of this gathering and applaud their efforts to provide you this experience at no cost."

Adam paused and drew a deep breath "Would everyone please join hands?"

Muffled commotion came from the direction of the crowd as over a million people tried to join hands. "Clouds will begin to form - please do not be alarmed - they are a product of the energy we are sharing together."

Adam paused again and looked skyward. The blue sky gave way to a high white haze which quickly thickened. The clouds grew dark and drooped closer to the ground. They swirled like a forming hurricane, but their pace was much slower and only a gentle warm breeze was felt on the ground. Before long, the sky was a deep purplish black in every direction. Then the swirling gradually stopped.

Adam shifted his gaze from the clouds to the crowd before him.

"Dear God! Look at that!" exclaimed Pastor Kanger to the others. They gasped along with the gathering at the appearance of a distinct golden halo around Adam's head. It was faint at first, but grew in intensity until it almost looked metallic.

Adam continued "In the past weeks I have shared God's word with you. Many of you have felt God's hand personally and lost the use of your legs. Later, the hand of God joined with each of you in a day of healing."

"God IS ALIVE!" exclaimed Adam "In each of us and in all things. If you look directly for God, your eyes will not find what you seek. Use your senses indirectly to understand that God is everywhere. You don't need to see the blue jay to know by his call that he is nearby. You don't need to see the lemon to know someone nearby has cut into one. You don't need to turn your head to identify a loved one talking to you - you know who they are from their voice. Open your senses to God's great voice! God is everywhere. From the tiniest things to the largest."

Chapter 23 - Adam Speaks

"At this moment, you feel the pull of gravity holding you to the earth. You can't see it, but you know it's there. Most of the time you forget about gravity, but it's always there, just the same. Feel the pull of God - it's always there, just like gravity. Your conscience is God's whisper - telling you what's right or wrong - what's wasteful or efficient. Listen . . . look . . . feel . . . you know God is there - you are never without God."

"God has made available to each of us some very special gifts. Starting with life itself, these gifts can be used to make the world a better place. Challenge one another - join with one another - find the ways you can contribute. Drop the artificial barriers society has created over the centuries - don't let property, wealth, religion, race, cultures, and the superficial aspects of life separate you. Place one of your hands in the hand of your neighbor and your other hand in the hand of God. Together you will be amazed at all the good you can do."

"A staggering gift we share is our ability to combine our reasoning skills with our ability of speech. This allows us to resolve conflicts through the power of our ideas instead of the power of physical force. When we resort to physical force, we demonstrate a poor use of our lives."

"One of the greatest gifts we have is our ability to make recordings of our knowledge and experiences. If we perform this task accurately, we can share our successes and our failures with one another. This sharing can happen today as well as in years to come. The result can be a society engaged in a lengthy continuous improvement process. We don't have to repeat the same mistakes. We can always do what we have learned is best. When we discover a new 'best', we can record that method for the benefit of others. We must be careful, however, to not distort the truth. If we do, people will begin to not trust what we record and will have to relearn much of what has already been done. Instead of moving forward and getting better, we will stagnate or slip back to some old wasteful habits."

"Remember the words you have heard and the sights you have seen. Share them with future generations so they will know, as you now know, that God is alive in each of us and our purpose in life is to do what we can to make things better."

Chapter 23 - Adam Speaks

Adam looked down at the stage floor and took a deep breath. He then glanced backwards slightly at Jamahl, Lisa, Pastor Kanger, and the author . . . and offered another gentle smile. He then turned to face the crowd.

Adam raised his arms and held his hands with his palms toward the sky. "And now, may the radiance of God's grace burn like a fire in each of you . . . now and forever more!"

The halo around Adam's head began to grow in size and become more like a bright aurora. The expanding halo extended over Adam's head and went behind him, down his back. When it reached his waist, the halo stopped growing and Adam began to rise from the stage. The glow of the halo and Adam were easy for all to see with the backdrop of the dark clouds and the rocks of the canyon. When Adam was about 30 feet above the stage, the halo began to grow once more, this time enveloping Adam completely, hiding even his outstretched arms. The halo cloud began to circulate with a rapid, random motion, reminiscent of models of electrons orbiting a nucleus. The golden glow quickly became white as the halo cloud bulged once more then exploded. An expanding ring of halo burst from where Adam had been and swept in all directions through the assembled crowd. Like the shock wave from a nuclear detonation, the energy field which was once Adam passed through everyone, providing a warm feeling as it passed. As the energy field reached the limits of the assembled people, it dissipated.

The millions were breathless. Many fell to their knees. Many hugged someone else. Most wept with tears of joy. The passing energy field had purified and charged each of them. All believed that God was real. Each had a new understanding of God and their personal potential to do many things to make the world a better place.

In a matter of minutes, the dark clouds lightened to gray, then white, then faded completely and gave way to bright, warm sunshine. It was as if God's smile was pouring down from the heavens.

The musicians scheduled to perform after Adam's segment, numbly found their way to the microphones and began to sing:

Chapter 22 - *A Day With God* - Performances

<u>Amazing Grace</u>

John Newton

Amazing grace!
How sweet the sound
That saved a wretch like me!
I was once was lost,
But now I'm found,
Was blind,
But now I see.

Twas grace that taught my heart to fear,
And grace my fears relieved;
How precious did that grace appear,
The hour I first believed.

Through many dangers, toils, and snares,
I have already come;
'Tis grace that brought me safe thus far,
And grace will lead me home.

When we've been there ten thousand years,
Bright shinning as the sun;
We've no less days to sing God's praise,
Than when we first begun.

Amazing grace!
How sweet the sound
That saved a wretch like me!
I was once was lost,
But now I'm found,
Was blind,
But now I see.

**God's
Gifts
To
Us All**

~ Chapter 24 ~

And Then . . .

Chapter 24 - And Then . . .

In the weeks that followed *A Day With God*, the world wrestled with what to do with what they had experienced. Most of the news reports dealt with some aspect of the reactions or implementation of the events surrounding Adam Sampson. Each of the millions who attended *A Day With God* continued to radiate an inner glow to everyone they met.

The hottest debates raged with the world's religious leaders. The recent events were hard to ignore. Many of the major religions were divided on the issue - one party holding dearly to the ancient manuscripts alone - the other side wanting to blend in the ancient writings along with the experiences of Adam Sampson. In several regions, a 'Sampsonite' religion emerged where followers largely ignored ancient writings altogether and focused their attention only on Adam Sampson and what they perceived as his teachings.

As the weeks became years, Dr. O'Connor and his wife teamed with Jamahl Washington to form an organization called *Partnerships For Urban Success*. The doctor made contacts with the wealthy and secured lines of funding. Jamahl and the doctor's wife joined forces to set up networks in most of the major urban areas. Jamahl made use of his inner city knowledge while Margaret unleashed her endless energy to coordinate efforts and to keep careful records. Sponsors were linked to their urban focus areas or focus families and blended selected direct funding with an accountability for results in the benefactors. Urban areas found their path to success through countless partnerships. Political solutions became unimportant in comparison and most were eventually abandoned.

Sue Bailey, who had healed Melissa Meyers of her burns, resigned from broadcasting. Initially she worked with the O'Connors and Jamahl Washington. Later, they all agreed to separate the financial efforts from the physical efforts. Sue created a new organization called *Exercise For A Better World*. As an alternative to health clubs, Sue's organization combined physical exercise with doing something positive for the community. In good weather trash was collected, trees were planted, gardens were made, and things were painted. In bad weather, structures of all sorts were cleaned and fixed. Most communities eventually had their own *Exercise For A Better World* as well as *Partnerships For Urban Success*.

Chapter 24 - And Then . . .

Author Michael Brown published the book as Adam had requested. The book quickly became the best-selling publication the world had known. It was translated into almost every language and provided a source of inspiration in every society. The author directed most of the royalties into rural areas and small cities. Large tracts of land were purchased for conversion into parks and nature areas. The author also made large personal donations into research to learn more about the physical world and how best to manage resources over the long term.

The promoters for *A Day With God* made a video about preparations for the event. Like most material claiming to have direct association with Adam Sampson, it was a best seller. Since the group made no effort to utilize their profits to make the world a better place, each suffered as Adam had predicted. Each died following prolonged suffering from a disease that the medical experts could not identify or control. Several members of their family suffered from the mystery disease as well with the same results.

Lisa Walters and Pastor Kanger were eventually married. They worked together on a feature film *God's Gifts To Us All* and used their royalties to work in foreign countries. There they shared their experiences and helped people find the same personal relationship with God that each of them had found.

For countless generations, the story was told time and time again. The books were read and the films were viewed. As society changed, the principles that Adam enumerated were adapted to the new technologies and social conditions. When man left the earth to colonize distant worlds, they took God with them.

Never again was there any doubt that God was alive. Those that elected to not follow God's way knew they did so with consequences. Those that did follow God's way lived lives filled with purpose and satisfaction. Little of their time was spent 'doing nothing'. They filled their days caring for others and making the most of their talents, resources, and ingenuity. They slept well every night and died with a sense of immense satisfaction with what they had done with their lives.

God's Gifts To Us All

~ Chapter 25 ~

And You . . .

Chapter 25 - And You . . .

This book is not about Adam Sampson. This book is not about God.

This book is about you.

What have you done today to make the world a better place? How about yesterday? What about tomorrow?

Cast aside your excuses.

Go find someone and tell them that you love them - show them that you care.

Clean something. Fix something.

Learn something and share it with everyone else.

Be honest in all you do and say. Be someone everyone else can always trust.

Get involved in your community. Show those around you that you know how to live. Teach future generations how to live.

Find the hand of God in all you see.

Be accountable for your life. Do something good with it.

God's greatest gift is YOU!

Be one with God . . .

Chapter 25 - And You . . .

Start

TODAY!

Chapter 25 - And You . . .

Think about . . .

**God's
Gifts
To
Us All**

. . . and make a difference with your life